The Matter of the

Bandersnatch Burglar
AND OTHER HEINZ NOONAN
IMPOSSIBLE CRIME SHORT STORIES

Steve Levi

Master of the Impossible Crime

PUBLICATION CONSULTANTS
WE BELIEVE IN THE POWER OF AUTHORS
PO Box 221974 Anchorage, Alaska 99522-1974
books@publicationconsultants.com, www.publicationconsultants.com

ISBN Number: 978-1-63747-100-5
eBook ISBN Number: 978-1-63747-101-2

Library of Congress Catalog Card Number: 2022936009

Manufactured in the United States of America

"If everyone's thinking the same thing then
no one is thinking."

. . . Heinz Noonan

THE MATTER OF THE BANDERSNATCH BURGLAR

Captain Heinz Noonan, the "Bearded Holmes" of the Sandersonville Police Department, was plowing through a mountain of paperwork searching for a case file that he could have sworn he had seen less than an hour earlier but was proving to be as elusive as the Bandersnatch Burglar – so-called because he, or she, left snatches of Lewis Carroll poetry on swatches in burgled homes – as the telephone in his administrative assistant's office kept up such a persistent ring he had no choice but to abandon his archaeological expedition forthwith and proceed with a frustrated air to the adjacent office to terminate the incessant jangle of the machine.

"Yeah?"

"Harriet?" It was a deep male voice, the kind that could be used as a foghorn if the Coast Guard ever abandoned LORAN.

"I don't think so but I'll check." He looked down at his trousers. "No, this isn't Harriet."

"Is Harriet there?"

"Not if I answered the phone."

"Where can I reach Harriet?"

"Since she's on vacation, I'd say Denver or Miami depending on what day it is."

"It's today," the voice boomed with a tint of annoyance. "What kind of a joker are you?"

"I thought I was a pretty good one. I'll transfer you back to the front desk and you can leave a message for Harriet."

"Don't you want to hear what I have to say?"

"I don't know. Do I?"

"This is Chief of Detectives Heinz Noonan, isn't it?"

"Yeah, who's this?"

"The Bandersnatch Burglar. At least that's what they've been calling me in the newspapers."

It was hard to catch Chief of Detectives Heinz Noonan by surprise but the call from the Bandersnatch Burglar had done exactly that.

"You're the Bandersnatch Burglar?"

"No, I'm the tooth fairy."

"Why are you calling me?" Noonan looked around for someone to signal so the call could be traced – until he realized Harriet had one of those incoming number displays on her phone. Noonan looked down the phone number as he spoke, his face registering consternation as he looked at the number, clearly trying to place it in his mind.

"To let you know you've got it all wrong."

"Wrong? I've got what wrong?" Now Noonan was searching for a pen or pencil in Harriet's desk, which did no good, first, because her desk was locked and second, because Harriet was a computer, FAX and email freak and treated hand-held writing implements as if they were tools of the devil. He finally dug a pencil out of his own trouser pocket and used the back of a day-by-day calendar to take notes.

There was a deep breath on the other end of the line. "The burglaries. I am not a burglar."

Now it was Noonan's turn to hold his breath. "You're the Bandersnatch Burglar and you aren't a burglar? Then what have you been doing burgling homes?"

"That's what I'm on the phone to talk to you about, Chief. It's OK if call you Chief, Chief?"

"Yeah, it'll do. I'm sorry but I must have missed something, Bandersnatch. I guess if you can call me Chief I can call you Bandersnatch, right?"

"Sounds fair to me. Look, Chief, I am not a burglar. I'm a filcher. I only steal things of no value."

"No value!? You've been doing pretty well lately. Pretty nifty stuff for not having any value. Like that Picasso and the Dali. Both originals."

"That's why I'm calling you, Chief. I'm just a scofflaw. Those jobs aren't mine."

Noonan registered surprise. He leaned back in Harriet's chair, the high top of the backrest catching his shoulder blades oddly. "What do you mean they're 'not your jobs?' You're the one who has been leaving enough Lewis Carroll swatches to make a quilt."

"Yeah, guess so. By the way, don't bother to trace this call. As I'm sure you know by now, I've got a scrambler that alters numbers on those call display devices. You recognize that phone number, eh?"

Noonan stared at the number and a thought line furrowed his brow. Clearly he couldn't place it. "What makes you think there is a call display screen on this phone?"

"Please, Chief. If you had a call display screen on your office phone, I would have called you there. But I had to settle for your admin assistant. Are you sure the number doesn't mean anything?"

"I'm not sure."

There was a silence for a moment. "Think, Chief, think."

Suddenly Noonan's face lit up. "That's my old phone number in Sandersonville! Why, that's twenty years old! How'd you get that number?"

"I'm a clever little person, Captain Noonan. Much too clever to be out burglarizing homes. Just to show you I know what I'm doing, do you recognize *this* number?"

As Captain Noonan watched, the numbers on Harriet's incoming call screen changed, the lights flashing as the number bars changed from his old home to his own office phone, the other instrument barely ten feet away. Noonan momentarily looked over his shoulder at his office as if he expected to see someone sitting there. "How did you do that?"

"Electronics, Chief, the magic of electronics. I do all kind of things. Like, I'll bet you think I'm a man, right?"

"From your voice, I'd say that's a good bet."

"Well, then listen to this. See what happens as I talk." Sure enough, as the Bandersnatch Burglar was speaking, the pitch of the voice raised until it became a tinny female voice, ragged on the edges as if the woman had just finished a long, hard day and was about to explode because the kids has spread a sheet of toys across the living room floor just before company arrived for dinner.

"That's amazing, Bandersnatch, but we're still back to the basic reason you called me."

"Like I said, Chief," the tinny woman's voice continued. "I'm not the burglar you are *really* seeking. In fact, I'm not a burglar at all. See, you've been following the wrong clues. Now, if you look at your case files for my jobs very carefully you will see all of the burglaries were different and the loot varied from cash to silver to paintings. But I'll bet you missed something that is similar with all of them – other than the swatches, of course."

"Like what?"

"Oh, something seemingly insignificant. I'll bet when you look at those police reports, you are going to see big, expensive items missing, and highly insured items. But you are not going to find something small and valueless that was stolen from each residence and not even listed as stolen."

"Why would anyone list anything that lacks a value as missing?" Noonan shook his head in confusion. "If it lacks value, it makes no difference if it gets stolen."

"Ex-actly, Captain Noonan. If you go back and re-interview the owners of the 15 burglaries you have been accusing me of perpetrating . . ."

"Fifteen? At last count there were only . . ."

"The day is young, Chief, the day is still young. There are two more thefts outstanding. One won't be reported for a day or two and the other until the middle of next week when the couple returns from Hawaii."

"But you just said you weren't a burglar."

"That's right. If the pattern holds, those two homes will be burgled as well, with me getting the blame for the jobs."

"Wait a minute." Noonan shook his head. "What you are telling me is someone has figured out your pattern and is burglarizing homes you have already, already, . . . what do you do if you don't burglarize the homes?"

"As I was about to say earlier, Chief, I'm a scofflaw. I steal things of no value. I don't need money so I do the B&E, as you call it, for a thrill. I snag things of no value and then leave."

"Like what?"

"Well, as I was saying before, if you re-check the residents of all of the burgled homes, you will find the victims probably didn't list everything that was missing. In fact, I'll bet quite a few of them don't even know one particular item is missing. You see, the reason I left the swatches was so the residents would know someone had been in their homes even though it may take them a while to figure out what was stolen."

"Now this is a bit hard for me to believe," Noonan said as he put his pencil away. "What you are basically saying is you break and enter homes and steal something of so little value no one will even know it's missing so you have to leave the swatches to let them know you've been there."

"Right on, Chief."

"Not only that, you're also telling me someone knows which homes you are entering and then burgles the homes after you leave. How would anyone know what homes you were going to break and enter unless you told them?"

"Now that's a good question, Chief. It's such a good question I don't have an answer for you. I think I know why though. See, to get into these homes, I have to cut through burglar alarm systems, get around dogs, short circuit security systems and things like that. Once I'm in, it's a cakewalk for whomever is doing the follow-up jobs. I've done all the brain work. All they have to do is follow in my footsteps, so to speak."

"Well that certainly follows. But that really has nothing to do with me."

"Oh, but yes it does. Your focus of attention that has to change. You've been chasing the wrong guy for the right reason. You are assuming I am pulling off the burglaries and leaving the swatches as a signature. That's a reasonable assumption. What I'm telling you is you're following the wrong scent. You want to catch the real burglars, not me. I want to help you do that."

Noonan laughed. "You want me to believe you want to help me catch someone to give you an alibi for all your B&E? How am I supposed to know you aren't really doing the burglaries yourself and just using me as a way to get a competitor out of the business?"

"Good question, Chief. My answer is in three parts. First, if I'm not who I say I am, why am I calling you?"

"Like you said earlier, that's such a good question I don't have an answer for it."

"Good. Second, if you check with the 13 home owners again, you will find there was a single, identical item that was stolen from all of them they did not report. How would I know what that one item was?"

"Good point. But then again, you haven't told me what that one item is."

"You should have no trouble getting verification after the first two or three people fess up. Finally, in answer to your last question, why do you care if I'm pulling your leg or not? If you catch the real burglars what do you care if you get some help from the underbelly of society? Once they're out of our hair, you can go on to other important cases and I can continue to be the scofflaw I am."

"You know I don't believe you."

"Oh, I'm sure you have your doubts," the voice said but it began to change again, modulating in pitch until the voice became a neutral, neither male nor female, with a slight reverberation as if it was coming from a sound chamber. "But you really don't have much choice, do you? Besides, Captain Noonan, Chief of Detectives, you like the challenge. After you check with the 13 home owners, pay a visit to 1898 Clara Nevada Street and 1979 John Hale Plaza. You'll need a locksmith to get into both of those locations because the owners are away on holiday. Then we'll be in touch."

"How will I know how to get in touch with you?"

"Silly boy, I'll be in touch with you."

True to his word, the Bandersnatch Burglar had been correct when he fingered two more burglaries. At 1898 Clara Nevada Street, the police arrived just as the aged couple who owned the home arrived, fresh from three days of vacation in the Napa Valley and concerned about the call they had received in the middle of the night for permission to enter their house. With a carload of fine wines, they were humored to find a contingent of detectives on their doorstep with a locksmith trying to get inside.

However, their humor turned quickly to grief when they discovered their home had been stripped of every item of high value despite the fact they had the most sophisticated burglar alarm system on the market – as well as a private security monitoring system and a rapid response hookup to the Police Department which appeared to be operational. Only after everyone got inside the house did they discover why the system had failed to alert the authorities: the interior monitoring had been cross-wired to a video tape machine that played a recording of the empty room for hours. Then, at the end of the tape, a switch transferred control of the security cameras back to the room scene. It was as if nothing had ever happened. The ultimate take-a-bite-out-of-crime equipment, a pair of Dobermans, were sound asleep in the living room courtesy, as it was later discovered, of a powerful sleeping potion which they had somehow taken internally. Probably in the form of a steak.

The booty was spectacular. In addition to a Modigliani original and a handful of late Dali prints, there was also a collection of rare historical documents including letters signed by George Washington, an IOU for Daniel Webster and other assorted documents signed by John Jay, John Adams, Elvis Presley, Harry Truman, Warren Sitka, and Julia Ward Howe. The usual collections of jewelry and silverware were also missing as was an antique desk chair and a collection of valuable porcelain plates. Whoever had taken the plates had known they were in the home as there were indications a box and packing material had been brought into the house. A swatch with a stanza from Lewis' Carroll's "Jabberwocky" was laid out in the center of the dining room table with a brandy snifter on top with some hardened, golden residue but no fingerprints. The couple was too distraught to think about small, valueless items that might be missing as well.

The scene at 1979 John Hale Plaza was much the same. The Clark family was located in Hawaii and gave the police permission to enter the estate. Once again, the home's security system had been adjusted to give the thief's time to make away with a fine collection of Ming dynasty vases, some Assyrian amphorae and an exquisite elephant tusk carving that exceeded six feet and was a complete scene of a procession in a marketplace in India. The bedrooms had been ransacked so it was assumed jewelry had been stolen and an empty space on a kitchen shelf indicated the probable theft of a silver set. A rug had been taken from a hallway, that clue provided by a faint square of double-sided tape that had held the material in place, and one of the walls had a large, discolored square indicating that something that had been hanging had been stolen, like a tapestry.

Once again, a Lewis Carroll swatch was prominent. This time it was on the seat of massive black oak office chair that had been swiveled out to block the entrance to the den. This swatch had a clip from "Phantasmagoria."

Back in his office, Noonan began the painstaking job of going over the police reports for the other 13 burglaries. Without the call from the Bandersnatch Burglar, it appeared all jobs were pulled by the same perpetrators. The entrance was clever and showed signs of superior knowledge of electronics. There was no damage to the premises and only the most valuable items were carted away. The thieves had had as much as four hours to as little as 75 minutes to pull off their capers and in most cases they were well away from the home by the time the residents returned. The closest call they had was the 75-minute robbery in which the owners returned from a party early and nearly caught the thieves red-handed. But the house was empty and all that there was to indicate someone had been there recently was one of the owner's Cuban cigars smoldering in the ashtray and had no ash column.

All homes had swatches of Lewis Carroll poetry, none of them repeats. The swatches were on black and green cotton, the kind of fabric that could be bought in any retail outlet, and the thread was generic as well. The print pattern clearly indicated a sophisticated embroidery system, but there were easily 30 such commercial establishments on the Outer Banks alone, many of them employing sweat shop operators who were reluctant to discuss anything with the police but the time of day, weather or how the red drum were running.

As there were also no indications of valueless objects being missing, Noonan made some phone calls. Each was a disappointment. First, no one believed he was calling about an object that had no value. Second, no one was interested in searching through their homes again for an object that had no value. Third, everyone wanted to know when the police were going to find their treasured items. Fourth and finally, if the police were so damn good, why didn't he know what he was looking for and if he didn't know, how were they supposed to? It was not a productive afternoon and evening.

The next morning proved no better. The couple from 1898 Clara Nevada filed their final report and were still too upset to talk about much. The family from 1979 John Hale Plaza arrived by noon and were doing inventory when Noonan walked through their front door for the second time in two days.

"You found our belongings?" the wife said in hopeful surprise.

"I'm afraid not," signed Noonan. "We're still working on it. But I do have a question or two if you have a moment."

"Well, we've already told your people everything we know. Can't you just read the reports?"

"Not for what I'm looking for. Can we sit down for a moment?"

The wife led Noonan to the dining room table where she served him a cup of coffee.

"Now, what can I do for you?"

"You seem to be taking this well."

"Am I?" The wife pushed a wayward hair back from her forehead. "I guess from the outside it must appear that way. Inside, well, we lost a lot of our life in that robbery, things we've been collecting for years. Valuable collectables. A lot of money went right out the front door."

"I'm sorry about that." Noonan coughed nervously for a moment. "I have a rather strange question for you and you might not be able to answer it today, maybe never. But I thought I'd try."

"That's an odd lead-up."

"Yes, it is, but it could be very important. Now, when you did an inventory of everything that was stolen did you leave anything off the list? Maybe there was something you didn't report because it was so small you didn't think it was worth your while to report or had so little value that you thought you might have misplaced it rather than it was stolen."

"Why would anyone want to steal something that had no value?"

"I don't have an answer for that. But it could be an important clue."

"No, I can't really think of anything that fits that bill. Everything that was stolen had a value. Will the answer help me get our property back?"

"There's a good chance it will."

"In that case I'll do another search. Do you have a card?" Noonan handed her a card and as he rose to leave, the wife was calling her kids. "The best person to look for something that has no value is someone who doesn't know the value of anything." She smiled as her two children, 5 and 9 years old, came into the room. "That describes my children perfectly," she said.

Noonan smiled.

An hour later he was smiling still for he had a list of ten objects of no value that had disappeared or been lost recently from 1979 Warren Sitka Plaza. Three phone calls later he had narrowed the list to a single object: a faux alabaster canopic.

At first he didn't know what a canopic was. It was one of those familiar terms, possibly Egyptian, but it was only after he looked it up on the internet that he remembered what it was. Yes, it had been Egyptian but its use has long since been abandoned. For about 3,000 years. A canopic was the jar into which the viscera of the deceased were placed before the embalming process began. The heart, lungs, intestines along with the various and sundry other internal organs were extracted from the cadaver and placed in the canopic so when the deceased was revivified – if that was the correct theological physiological term for the ancient Egyptians – the blessed individual would be able to breath, digest, pass gas and urinate in the next life.

The most common form of canopics, as Noonan discovered, was in a set of four. Often they appeared as busts of the individual, four of them, two sets of two facing each other nose-to-nose, in a stone chest. (Noonan enjoyed that pun.) Made out of calcite, which was better known as Egyptian alabaster, the jars could hold about 10 gallons of innards.

Of interest to both Noonan and clearly the scofflaw, the style of canopic changed over the years. By the Eighteenth Dynasty, the canopics no longer appeared as elaborate vessels topped with human heads. Sometimes there were heads of gods – baboon, hawk and falcon – as well as a human head. The composition of the canopics changed as well. While calcite was still being used, so was wood, pottery, limestone and even a more common stone. Eventually they became solid, symbolic of their previous function.

The canopics that were missing were of a latter vintage, from the 25th Dynasty. This canopics were basically solid weights. They were all about the same size, between two and three feet high. Some were made of wood while others were made of calcite. Of particular interest to Noonan, all of the canopics that were stolen had been snatched from the traditional group of four. In only three of the burglaries were the faux canopics in the same locations. In the balance of the burglaries, the four figures were scattered around the house. One had been used as a bedroom doorstop while another was used to fill an odd corner in an otherwise cluttered office. But only one of the figures was missing from each home: the falcon.

If the scofflaw was telling the truth and all he was really taking was the faux falcon canopic, there really wasn't any way to prosecute him. The canopics had no value and even if a search found all of them in a single place in his residence, there was no way to prove that any one of them, or for the matter, all of them, came from burgled homes. Even fingerprints of the owners on the canopics were not enough. They could have handled the canopics anywhere because they could have been purchased anywhere.

Could the Bandersnatch Burglar be telling the truth?

"You found the items, didn't you?" It was a strange voice on Noonan's line, electronically male with a pronounced brogue.

"Pardon?"

"You found out about the items, right? The ones I stole?"

"Ah, Bandersnatch. Maybe."

"Don't lie to me, Chief. I have my sources. You did pop open two more burglaries and that must have made you look good at headquarters."

"No, actually it made me look very bad. You don't get credit for reporting burglaries; you get credit for solving them. Now I'm being harassed for not solving the burglaries I'm reporting."

"Well, work with me and we'll solve these crimes together."

"That's the rub here, as you know. I can't very well work with someone who's doing B&E to catch a burglar."

"Takes a thief to catch a thief. Besides, why should you care? You've got snitches. I'm just another one."

"It doesn't work like that, Bandersnatch. You see, if I catch the perps who are doing the jobs, then I've got to sit on the witness stand and say where I got the lead to snag them. What am I supposed to say, that I just pulled their name out of thin air?"

"You just say you got lucky."

"Judges don't like it when you lie."

"You're not lying, you're just saying you got an anonymous tip. Or do some prelim groundwork to cover your tracks. Come on, Captain. You've been in the law enforcement business for more than three decades. You're telling me you don't know how to develop leads that are fruitful for court appearances? You probably won't have to worry about it anyway because if you catch them red-handed, they'll cope a plea so you won't ever see the inside of a courtroom on this matter."

"So you say. A lot could go wrong. What about you? You know the moment they get fingered; they'll know you did it. That's bad news for your health."

"Maybe, but they're putting me at risk now."

Noonan was silent for a long moment, so long Bandersnatch coughed nervously on the other end of the line. That might have been a mistake because the cough was definitely masculine, which Noonan dutifully recorded in a notebook he had open on his desk.

"Now, I'm afraid to ask this, but how do you suggest we work together?"

"Well, I've been pretty careful lately. I've got a choice of targets and I haven't decided which one to hit next. When I do, I'll let you know after I'm inside. I won't be in very long so you won't catch me. But, with any luck, you'll catch the other perps on the inside after I leave."

"Why should I believe you?"

"Why should you care?" came the response. "You're going to get the real perps and get lots and lots of credit."

"That really doesn't solve anything," Noonan retorted. "As soon as another swatch shows up, the press will be on me like white on rice."

"Captain, pl-ease. If you have to use a simile, at least use a good one. Why not 'a cheap suit in the rain,' or 'dimples on a golf ball.'"

"That still leaves us facing the same bear in the trail. If you are telling me the truth and I do capture these perps, the minute you leave the next swatch, the bad guys are going to say they were not responsible for the all the other burglaries, only the one where they were caught. If you do pull off another burglary and snatch a falcon canopic, everyone is going to know I didn't get the real Bandersnatch Bandit at all. I'll be the laughing stock of the city even though I caught the burglars. Even if you tell me you're going to stop pulling off scofflaw burglaries, how am I to know you're not going to go on vacation and come back in a year and start all over again?"

"That's all very true," Bandersnatch said. "All of it. Yes, you do have a problem because I am not planning on stopping snatching the falcon canopics or leaving the swatches. But you're very clever guy, Chief of Detectives Heinz Noonan. That's why I'm calling you."

"So you want me to solve your public relations problems?"

"In a word, yes. I want to get the credit I deserve as a yegg of falcon canopics of no value, a scofflaw, and a second story man who leaves Lewis Carroll swatches."

"Well, you can't be a second story man because half the homes you've burgled don't have second stories."

"Good point. Then just call me a cat burglar of falcon canopics. I don't care. Just get the professionals off my amateur back."

With that the Bandersnatch Burglar hung up the phone.

The problem facing Noonan was most perplexing. There was, unfortunately, some merit to the Bandersnatch Burglar's claim. It did appear as if there were two sets of thieves at work; or at least one scofflaw and a band of clever professionals. The fact a falcon canopic had been stolen from every location clearly indicated a pattern. That the canopics were virtually worthless indicated a scofflaw was probably involved. The balance of the loot from the homes was varied and there did not seem to be any significant pattern of thievery. Just that it was carefully chosen and high end.

There were some unusual angles to the burglaries. First, they were all in what could reasonably be called 'high security' residences. These were not middle class B&Es. That meant someone had to really know what he – or she – was doing to get into the homes. Second, the spread of loot of was so wide it was hard to see how it could be fenced. Many of the items were one-of-a-kind: a personal letter signed by George Washington, a Modigliani original, an antique pinky ring, an antique jade writing desk and other items like that. These items could only be sold to a collector. But when it comes to a unique item, in most cases it is the buyer who contacts the thief not the other way around. If the burglaries were truly targets of opportunity, the thieves were ending up with a lot of high end goodies with no place to sell them. This meant they were not making a lot of money. They had lots of assets they could not sell and no cash to pay the bills.

Third, and most perplexing, it was hard to believe the Bandersnatch Burglar did not know who the perps were. This burglar had pulled off more than a dozen jobs and every one of them had been followed by a real burglary.

Every one of them.

Even if he acted alone he had to know he was leaking information somewhere. Anyone who was smart enough to play electronic games with the telephone system was smart enough to figure out who was raining on his parade.

Assuming he did know, why did he care? The scofflaw was getting what he wanted – though God knew why he wanted to collect falcon canopics – so why should he care if he was being followed about by capitalists? This was all quite baffling to Noonan and made no sense whatsoever. Making even less sense is what he was supposed to do about it. He couldn't realistically arrest the perps and let the scofflaw go even if the scofflaw was only stealing valueless items. But he couldn't ignore the robberies either.

The next time the scofflaw called, Noonan was prepared.

"Well," said the voice, a high pitched teenager this time, "have you decided to help me?"

"I don't see that I've got too much choice."

"I'm happy you see it that way."

"But you do know I'm going to have to arrest you too."

"You've got to catch me first. Just because I'm helping you catch the real bad boys and girls doesn't mean I'm giving myself up."

"Right. All right. Humor me. How can you have pulled over 15 spectacular robberies and have someone follow in your footsteps every time? You've got to know you have a leak somewhere in your organization."

"Good point, Captain. I thought about that as well. But, first, I'm the only one in my organization. Second, as I'm sure you have checked, there are seven major security firms in Sandersonville and I've hit residences monitored by all of them. So that ends any chance of an inside leak. Third, I don't talk in my sleep. Even if I did, I live alone. Fourth, I sweep my home and office regularly for bugs and I have yet to find one. I'm not sure how they know what I'm going to do. But they do."

"Could they be following you, waiting for you to make a move and then following up after you leave a residence?"

"Quite possibly."

"Let's take this from the top, shall we. How do you choose which residence to hit?"

"That's a little personal, isn't it?"

"Not if I'm going to help you."

"Fair enough. I hack into the sales records of companies who would most likely sell canopics. That gives me the names and addresses of people who have bought the item. Sales records are not secured or encrypted because they have no value. I have a long list and I choose my targets at random."

"How do you know that the canopics are actually there?"

"I don't. I just assume they are. So far I've been lucky."

"Well, they are too big to hide."

"Why would anyone want to hide a three-foot tall, fake canopic?" the voice of the Bandersnatch Burglar changed pitch to that of an old man. "That's what makes them so easy to steal. There is no reason to hide them. They cost a few hundred dollars so no one's going to get rid of them but they are still not worth very much."

"So," Noonan said as he wrote on his notepad, "you don't case a residence before you burgle it. You just know which home you want to enter, steal the electronic information for the security system and enter the house."

"Weeeelll, you're making it sound easier than it is. But, yeah, that's about right."

"How do you know that the people will be out?"

"Oh, I put a small camera focused on the house for a few days. You know, hidden in a tree or shrub. Then I just watch and see what happens. It doesn't take long to figure out the family's schedule. Then I'm in and out."

"Are you in and out fairly quickly?"

"No longer than ten minutes. Sometimes on the range of three or four minutes."

"When you leave, do your re-set the alarm?"

"Not the way you think. I don't turn off the alarm to enter so it isn't necessary to turn it back on when I leave. Basically I create an electronic time gap in the system and use the time gap to enter and leave. That way, when the tape is reviewed, there is no indication the alarm system has been breached. There is just an electronic jumble on the screen that appears to last a few seconds when, in fact, it has lasted 20 minutes."

"Can't the security people tell that from the time code?"

"Not really. The electronic gap also distorts the time sequence. After the apparent few seconds of distortion, the clock automatically restarts at midnight. There's no way to know that anyone has been in the residence."

"So the perps use your entrance through the electronic shield. But they have to take longer than 20 minutes."

"They just shut off the system. Then they turn it on after they leave. The clock resets itself and the security companies are not the wiser. That's why the perps have not been caught on tape."

"Have you ever seen anyone after you've burgled a residence?"

"Nope. I'm in and out."

"This is a most perplexing case."

"Oh, I figured you would appreciate it. Now, I am going to be in and out of a residence next Tuesday night. What I am going to do is tell you the minute I am out and gone. If you are clever you should be able to catch the thieves in the act."

"What makes you think they don't know you are dealing with us?"

"I don't. But if I make it into and out of the house quickly and you get there right away, the perps are going to be caught in the act. If they do not turn up, I'll leave a swatch and then the story will get out a scofflaw is loose in the city. As the story of the missing canopics spreads, the public will understand there are two sets of burglars out there – and I'm not the bad guy."

"I see. So, I should be here, at this number, for your call Tuesday evening."

"That's right. You should be able to make it to the burgled residence in about six minutes."

"I'll wait for your call."

True to his word, on Tuesday night, the Bandersnatch Burglar gave a call to Noonan's office. He gave an address on Wilford Circle and was off the phone. Ten minutes later the Sandersonville Police Department was arresting a gang of five men and four women who were looting the residence of a dotcom mogul who was skin diving off the coast of Mexico. They were caught red-handed, loading expensive antique furniture and Persian rugs into a battered moving van. The seven were moving quickly but methodically, like the professional movers they were. From the size of the loot and how they were packing the van Noonan figured they could have been in and out in less than an hour. They even brought drop clothes for the furniture. Noonan found three of the set of four canopic jars in the entryway, the falcon missing. The swatch, this time with a stanza from "The Hunting of the Snark," was on the kitchen table with a note that read "Thanks!"

As the Bandersnatch Burglar had stated, the electronic gurus at the Police Department did find the source of the glitch in the program.

"This was one very clever guy," said Lt. Samuelson as he looked through the programming spread sheet. "If he hadn't told you what he was doing, heck, we might never have found it."

"That was the plan, Samuelson. That was the plan."

"What do you mean?"

"Come on. We've got one more arrest to make."

To say the Bandersnatch Burglar was surprised when Noonan showed up at his doorstep was an understatement.

"I presume you are here to thank me for my help?"

"Yes, and to arrest you for burglary."

"Oh, that's rich. Don't you mean petty theft? Those canopic jars aren't worth much – even if you can find them on my residence."

"That's what confused me at first," Noonan replied. "Your story had more holes than a wall of chicken wire. It only made sense if I believed what you said. You were counting on your personality to fool me."

"Well, what did I get out of the robberies?"

"Cash," replied Noonan. "Lots of cash. The one sticking point in this entire case is what happened to the loot. Everything that was stolen was very high end, not the kind of things you would find in a pawn shop. Since the robberies were supposedly at random, the thieves could not have been stealing for a specific buyer. So where was the loot going? The answer, of course, is it wasn't going anywhere. The robberies were being done for the insurance money."

"But no one's property has been returned."

"How would you know that unless you were involved? And that, my dear Bandersnatch Burglar, is enough cause to have you arrested." Noonan turned to Lt. Samuelson, "Cuff him and read him his rights."

"You can't do this!" shrieked the burglar in his normal voice, that of a 50-year old man who appeared more as an outraged accountant than a criminal mastermind.

Samuelson droned through the Miranda rights and then nodded for a sergeant to take charge of the prisoner.

"You can't do this," the burglar shrieked. "I'm a scofflaw!"

"No," said Noonan, "you are not. How did you know no one's property had been returned? Because you work for the insurance industry. You didn't hack into any one's sales records to see who bought canopic jars, you knew what was being insured because you had the paperwork on your desk. You also knew where everything was in the homes that were burgled because you had seen pictures of the valuables, a requirement for the special kinds of insurance that would be needed for exquisite antiques and one-of-a-kind collectables. You didn't have to hack into any electronics either. You just installed the glitch while you were examining the security systems at the security companies. What did you do, convince them you had to look over the system before you would insure the homes they were watching? Why I'll bet those minimum wage guards could have cared less as you pawed through the system."

"But, but, but . . ."

Samuelson watched the burglar struggle as he was loaded into the back of a patrol car.

"That was most impressive, Chief," he said. "But how did you know where to find him?"

"It wasn't hard," Noonan replied. "Everything depended on me believing the scofflaw was stealing canopic jars. It was a tempting thought because it was so unusual. But there wasn't a dime of truth in it. So I followed the money. There was only one entity that could profit from robberies of this kind: insurance companies. If they could get back the purloined merchandise at less than the cost of the claim, they'd jump at the deal."

"But we checked out the insurance companies for the 13 robberies. They were all different!"

"Yes. But not the appraisers. There are not that many appraisers for this kind of high-end merchandise in Sandersonville. Noonan wagged his head knowingly. "Eighteen of them, as a matter of fact."

"Eighteen? How did you know which one was the bad apple?"

"I didn't," replied Noonan with a wicked smile. "But right now twelve of them and their families are having a free dinner at my favorite restaurant, Lorenzo's." Noonan leaned forward and smiled conspiratorially. "You see, they all think they've won the meal through some kind of a lottery. Three are out of town, one is sick and one is at an art exhibit as we speak. The eighteenth left his home and went to Wilfred Circle." He smiled stoically, "You see, I've been keeping track of them all."

"So the swatches were all a sham, a red herring."

"That's right," sighed Noonan. "Everything was made to make it appear there were two different robberies happening at the same time. I'm sure that was the plan all along."

"I don't understand," Samuelson was shaking his head.

"The original plan was to plant the swatches at each burglary and steal a falcon canopic. The appraiser would arrive when the thieves entered the premises, take the canopic and leave. He was never involved in the actual burglary so he could never be caught. But he provided the thieves with a list of valuables to steal, just different enough to keep him from becoming a suspect. But the thieves always made sure to steal a falcon canopic and leave a swatch. If they ever got caught, the stolen canopic jar and swatches were going to be their ticket to a short prison sentence. If they got arrested, the next time a canopic jar was stolen and a swatch was discovered, the perps could claim they were being charged with someone else's crime."

"I see," replied Samuelson. "Reasonable doubt."

"Correct! But our perps were too subtle for their own good. No one noticed the canopic jars were missing. So someone had to call the police. That's why I got the call."

"Well, that explains everything but where the loot is."

"That will be the easiest to find. We'll have it all before dawn. As soon as our gang of movers finds out they were being double-crossed, they'll spill every bean in the pot."

"What if they don't talk?"

"Then we'll just check warehouse space rented by our friend the appraiser over the last year. It shouldn't be that hard. The rental has to be large and indoor. It was probably safest to rent it in his name. That way if he was caught he could say he was dealing with the thieves on behalf of the insurance companies and arranging a quiet settlement. I'll bet he's already been accepting cash from the insurance companies to recover the stolen property quickly and quietly."

"Is there any way to get him?"

"I hope so. The record of vehicles into and out of the storage yard should convict him. I'll bet the drop-offs were made late at night, after the robberies. I'll bet we'll even find the van was in long term storage near the rental room. That way the thieves could hide the van and the loot at the same location."

Samuelson shook his head. "They almost got away with all of it. If the burglar hadn't of been so greedy, they would all have gotten away with it. I mean, who was going to stop them?"

"Greed, my dear Samuelson," replied Noonan. "The Bandersnatch Burglar never intended to share. This was to be the last burglary. He was using the master plan to have his gang arrested. They'd be sitting in jail cells while he was flying the coop. When we search his home I'll bet we find a stash of traveler's checks and a ticket to some location where the United States has no extradition treaty. If we hadn't nabbed him tonight, he'd have been in Rio by the time we connected the dots."

"Well, we certainly are lucky you were on the job. Was there any one thing that tipped you off?"

"I don't know if it was tip off or not. When I found the falcon canopic was the one being stolen, I mused that if I couldn't solve the case, people were going to be laughing at me for years. That got me to thinking about the old expression that he who laughs last laughs best. That was when I figured out there was less to this story than I was being told."

With that Noonan started walking toward his car. "If I'm really lucky," he said over his shoulder, "I can make it to Lorenzo's before my children finish off all the *fettucini Alfredo.*"

THE MATTER OF THE CLODHOPPER DELUGE

Captain Noonan, the "Bearded Holmes" of the Sandersonville Police Department was stuck on five letter word for German cars ending in "s." The closest he could come was "Benz" which did not, alas, end in an "s." Personally he could have cared less which German cars ended in "s." But his wife did. And she was going to call after her *Bridge Club Soiree* which, oddly, was in the afternoon, even though *soirees*, from the French, are in the evenings. The clue being the term *soir*, in French, for "evening."

He was so intent on contemplating the German car possibilities he failed to look at the incoming call notification reading on his electronic Beelzebub, the tool of Satan which both his wife and his commissioner demanded he keep with him at all times. As his commissioner was, blessedly, in Virginia Beach at some publicity gathering, that left his wife with the only one with his cell number – and in the case of Noonan – *cell* had a double meaning.

"The closest I can come to a five-letter word for German cars is Benz but it only has four letters."

"Add an 's,'" a strange woman's voice said. "In crossword puzzles, when it asks for a plural, automatically add an 's.' That reduces the letters to four and thus Benz fits."

"Great," said Noonan as he rubbed out the BMWs and the scratch paper on his desk and then looked at the incoming call notification. It was his wife's *Mephistopheles*. "Why do you have my wife's phone?"

"She told me to call. This is Rachel Bangladesh, spelling just like the country with none of the problems. I'm at the *Bridge Club Soiree* in Nags Head and mentioned an odd occurrence to your wife and she told me to call."

"OK," Noonan rolled his eyes. He could just imagine what was coming next. A missing cat? Or someone stealing a spare tire from her garage. "I see. And what is this strange occurrence."

"I volunteer at the Nags Head Value Village and Thrift Shop. Someone stole all of our shoes."

This was certainly a first for Noonan. Shoes in a thrift shop? What were shoes in a thrift shop worth? Couldn't you buy a pair for two or three dollars? That's not a lot of street value.

"Your shoes?"

"Yes. You know, the shoes we have for sale. Someone broke into the thrift shop one night and stole all the shoes."

"Just the shoes?"

"That's all we could find that was missing."

"Are we are talking about a break-in or did someone come in a shoplift the shoes?"

"Oh no, it was a break-in. We came in one morning last week and all the shoes were gone."

"Do you have any kind of security on the store?"

"Not the way you mean it. We don't have top notch security because we remove all the money every night. The rest of the store is just clothes. We keep a weak lock on the back door because we get broken into so often. Usually it's a homeless person looking for a warm place to spend the night and a place to get a free jacket or pair of pants. We're accustomed to homeless people looking for shelter we have a cheap door and a cheaper lock on the back door. We don't want to ruin a $100 door because someone wanted a jacket we got for free and are trying to sell for $3."

"But no security camera?"

"Why? There isn't anything of value in the store. We are a thrift shop, you know."

"Just the shoes?"

"Just the shoes."

"Any particular sizes?"

"All sizes. They just swept clean four shelves: children's, men's, women's, boots, high heels and tenny sneakers."

"How many pair we talking about?"

"All totaled, maybe 40."

"So, cash wise, you are out about $150."

"If we sold them, yes."

Noonan was silent for a moment. "Give me your phone number and I'll see what I can do."

Shoes? Noonan muttered to himself as he wrote down Bangladesh's number.

Then things got odder.

Since he didn't know anything about thrift stores, he put a call into someone who did:" Omar Zeffirelli. Zeffirelli was the owner of a small mall in Sandersonville – and aren't all the malls in Sandersonville small? – and asked about thrift thefts.

"Seriously? Well, Captain. It is Captain, isn't it."

'No. Not until there's a crime. Until then it's Heinz."

"Ok, Heinz. How much do you know about the thrift business?"

"It's for people who have very little money who need things very badly."

"Good enough. Yes, that's a good description of our clients. Thrift stores do not make money. They are not in the business of making money. They are in the business of keeping poor people alive. I donate the space for the Sandersonville Thrift Mart and cover water and sewer charges. I'm betting electricity and gas are donated . . . and solid waste. Everything in the Thrift Mart has been donated. The only real-world expenses are the employees. There is no money to be made in the thrift business."

"Is stealing from a thrift shop unusual?"

"Shoplifting is probably as common as in other stores. I don't know but I'm guessing the employees turn a blind eye to a lot of it. I mean, the people doing the shoplifting really need the jackets, shoes and whatever they abscond with. Wasting police and court time on a homeless shoplifter is probably not worth anyone's time so the blind eye…"

"Maybe," Noonan said and then added. "But in this case, the theft is four shelves of shoes."

"Pardon?"

"Shoes. Four shelves of shoes. Someone broke into the Nags Head Value Village and Thrift Shop and stole about 40 pair of shoes."

"Why?"

"That's what I thought you could tell me?"

"I can't think of a reason anyone would want 40 pair of old shoes. The best I can do is tell you to call the North Carolina Thrift Association. In Raleigh. They might know because I sure don't."

The Director of the North Carolina Thrift Association thought Noonan was kidding.

"Someone stole 40 pair of shoes. Why?"

"I was hoping you could tell me?"

"Is this a gag call?"

"No, actually. I really am Captain Noonan of the Sandersonville Police Department and this is an official call."

"Wow! OK. I, we, don't know anything about any theft of shoes. And I can't think of reason anyone would steal used shoes."

"Any other thrift shops in North Carolina report thefts?"

"Not as far as I know. But then again, if someone stole something from a store it would be reported to the local police, We would never hear about it."

"How many thrift stores are part of you association?"

"67, but they are not all thrift stores the way you probably think of them."

"But you are in touch with your members?"

"Of course."

"Will you send out an email asking if any of them have had thefts?"

"I can. Sure. Anything else?"

Noonan thought for a moment. "Yes, as a matter of fact. Ask if anything unusual has happened over, say, the last month."

"What do you mean by 'unusual?'"

"Out of the ordinary, odd, strange. I don't know. Hopefully one of your members will have a clue to why someone would steal 40 pairs of used shoes."

"You're the boss."

"I like your attitude. Here's my office email."

Three days later Harriett came into Noonan's office with three sheets of paper. She kind of/sort of held them against her chest and leaned forward with a humorous gleam in her eyes. "Tell me, oh, 'Bearded Holmes,' what a stuffed alligator, 15 beach towels, 16 used baseball caps, 30 brassieres, two dozen t-shirts, a dozen pair of pants of different sizes have to do with 15 pair of men's underwear and 30 pair of men's and women's socks – and," Harriet waggled the sheets of paper, "enough children's clothing to start a nursery have in common?"

Noonan thought for moment and then muttered, "Methodist Spring Break?"

"Very funny," Harriet sniped. "And I'm a recovering Methodist. Or is it an Episcopal? I can't remember. No, it's a list sent over by Omar Zeffirelli. I didn't know you knew him."

"I don't. But then again, this is Sandersonville. It's a small town and everyone knows everyone else's business even if they've never met."

"Another ha-ha. That's all that's on this list. Nothing else."

"I guess I have to give him a call."

"Good idea. And ask if he's a Methodist."

Zeffirelli might have been a Methodist but since Noonan didn't ask, Harriet would never know the answer. The answer Noonan was seeking was "what's with the list you sent over?"

"Odd, isn't it."

"An understatement. What am I looking at?"

"I don't know, to be honest. I got a phone call from the Director of the North Carolina Thrift Association. She didn't believe you were really who you said you were so she sent an email out and got this list. But she sent it to me because, . . ."

"Yeah," Noonan shook his head. "She doesn't know me from blue cheese."

"That's not the way I would have said it but, yeah. But there's an unusual wrinkle in this list. It's not things that have been stolen. It's a list of the things the same people have been buying."

"Sorry?"

"I had a long talk with the Director. When it comes to crime, as in theft, other than the usual shoplifting, there has been zip in the last year. And the year before that. No one could even remember a theft. But when she asked about odd occurrences – you asked her to ask that, right?"

"Yes."

"When it comes to oddities, a lot of thrift shops had the same answer. The oddity was not so much *what* was bought as *who* was buying it."

"I guess I missed that."

"Apparently there are two men, quite noticeable, who have been making unusual purchases. That's the list I sent you."

"What do you mean by 'noticeable?'"

"According to the director, one is a black man about 6' 7" and the other is short Chinese man, maybe five feet tall. The Chinese man speaks no English but the black man appears to be fluent in Chinese."

"How do they know the short man is Chinese?"

"I don't know. The general consensus was the short man was Chinese. They appeared together and the Chinese man picked out the product. The black man was there as a translator."

"It's an odd list of items?"

"I agree. What do you think in happening?"

"Not a clue.

"I don't see a crime here."

"Not yet," Noonan answered. "Not yet." And just as he said the last "not yet," a distant bell pealed in his psyche.

Whenever Noonan had a problem to solve, an unsolvable problem, he let it slip into the back of his mind where it could ferment. There are no unsolvables when it comes to the crime so it is only took a matter of time to solve the unsolvable. The importance was solving the unsolvable before time runs out.

Since there was no "Square One" to return to – the usual crime solving technique for detectives – Noonan had to do some off-the-wall thinking. The only common link was who was doing the buying. OK, well, what was the commonality of the items being bought. Just as important, were these two responsible for theft of the shoes or was that someone else? Good question. Assuming the shoes were stolen by the black and Chinese men, why steal the shoes if you bought everything else?

The only answer Noonan could come up with was the two men had run out of time for whatever they were planning on doing.

Suddenly there was a ticking clock.

But for what?

Noonan had long known almost all crimes end up being about money.

So where was the money link here?

He was still mulling over the list – a stuffed alligator? – that evening when his wife dragged him to a high school choral presentation. It was part of the SSS, Support Sandersonville Students, and as much as he hated gatherings, he always had time for the young. Afterall, when he became old and gray, the youth of today were going to be running the country he and his generation had run into the ground.

The choral presentation included some Costal North Carolina ballads including *The Ole Tar River*, which Noonan had never heard:

> Way down in North Car'lina,
> On the banks of the Ole Tar River,
> I go from there to Alabama,
> For to see my ole Aunt Hannah.

> Now Nancy, I must leave you,
> Do not let our parting grieve you,
> Dance and sing, forget your sorrow,
> I'll be back sometime tomorrow.

By the time the chorus hit "sometime tomorrow," the bell in Noonan's skull was reverberating loud enough to keep him awake for the rest of the program.

"You're a detective so I'm not going to ask how you knew about the pair?"

"I'm psychic," Noonan said off handedly. "Tell me about them?"

The manager of the Sandersonville dock shook his head. "Nothing illegal, if that's what you are asking about. They are the face of a company out of Hong Kong that owns a lot of properties in the area: warehouse space, parking lots, car rentals. In most cases they are the money behind the locals. The black man clearly speaks Chinese fluently and he's the one who handles all of the details with the local businesses. From the way they act, the Chinese man comes across as a stumblebum. You know, kind of the odd child who has strange ideas so they sent him as far from the family business as they could."

"Sandersonville is a long from Hong Kong. What do you mean by strange ideas?"

"Well, he wanted to open a video store, which might have been a money-maker a decade ago but not today. So it failed, to no one's surprise. Then it was high end furniture and there are already a dozen of those stores in Greenville, so the store went belly-up. Then an exclusive liquor store which went under and now it's a tour boat operation."

"Tell me about the tour boat operation."

"Nothing illegal, if that's what you are asking. The Chinese man bought an old boat, and I do mean old, real old, and cleaned it up. Everyone at the marina here knew it was a relic and hardly seaworthy, but the Chinese man bought it anyway. Put a lot paint on the outside and not a dime of improvement on the inside. He takes it out like clockwork every weekend. Down the Tar River. Some of the other boaters have seen him in Pamlico Sound so he's made it that far east."

"You said his is a tour boat operation. Does he have clients?"

"That I don't know. My guess is 'no.'"

"Why not?"

"A bunch of reasons but it's just a guess."

"Humor me."

"OK. He doesn't advertise anywhere I've seen and I'm in the business. Second, I've never seen anyone get on or off the *Elizabeth City.*"

"That's the name of the boat?"

"Yeah. Used to be the *Forget Me Knot*, 'not' spelled with a 'k.' It's bad luck to change the name of boat."

"In more ways than one."

"OK. You want more reasons?"

"Sure."

"I've never seen him in a bait shop and no one at the marina have seen him with fishing gear. He's not the sailing type or the fishing type or the tourism type. He's just, well, just a guy who gets in a boat once a week and sails down to Pamlico Sound by himself for whatever reason I do not know. The only thing I've seen him load onto the boat are boxes"

"Boxes?"

"Cardboard. About two at a time. I don't know what's in them but it's not food because he never has any clients I have seen."

"The black man never goes with him?"

"Never seen him on the boat. Always on shore. Sharp man. I'd say he's kind of the business body guard for the loser son. Speaks the language the Chinese man doesn't. Translator as opposed to a business partner."

"I see. One more question, is the *Elizabeth City* out today?"

"Left this morning. Odd thing, now that you ask about the boat. I saw the owner with a life preserver."

"Nurk? I've never heard the term." There was a look of confusion on the North Carolina State Trooper's face. "What does that term have to do with the shipwreck?"

"*Nurk*, Captain, is an old English term. The best translation today is the 'runt of the litter.' The worst of the litter and the last to be sold."

"And that has to do with the wreck of the *Elizabeth City*?" He ended the line with a lift indicating he expected more.

"There will be no wreck of the *Elizabeth City*. It's a scam about to occur."

"Let me get this straight, you're reporting a wreck before it happens? And if it's a boat, the Coast Guard will be the first on the scene."

"True, true," Noonan added. "But this is an insurance scam. I'm betting the boat wreckage will appear within a day or two and there will be a widespread search for survivors. None will be found and the owner of the *Elizabeth City* will file an insurance claim."

"But if there were people on board, they will have families who will end up suing the owners of the *Elizabeth City*."

"There were no people on board. Like I said, it was a scam. It is just a money-making scheme by the nurk of a Chinese family in Hong Kong. The guy has failed at every idea he's had. So he went big time for his last hurrah. My bet, he's out of the country by now. He took the *Elizabeth City* out onto Pamlico Sound and sank it. The surface is going to be littered with debris – clothing, shoes, baseball caps – and that's supposed to fool the Coast Guard into believing there were people on board. When the search finds no one, the boat will be declared a total loss and the Hong Kong company will collect insurance. No passengers means no lawsuits. It's just a scam."

"I see his lordship, our Commissioner of Homeland Security, has made the paper again." Harriet folded the *Sandersonville Express* to the front-page article and handed it Noonan. "Seems he and he alone broke up a Chinese extortion ring."

"Really?" Noonan did not bother to look at the paper.

"Odd," Harriet said with a false look of confusion on her face. "Not a single word about his staff. Us. Just that he – and he alone – broke up the extortion ring."

"Well, a 'ring' is one thing so I guess you could say one person is a 'ring.'"

"You could. But not the way he's said it," Harriet tapped the paper with her right index finger. "And it says he – and he alone – saved hundreds of thousands of dollars on a futile search for survivors of a wreck that never happened."

'All in a day's work," Noonan said as he smiled.

"Let me guess; the debris was all that stuff in the list I gave you last week."

"Probably."

"Probably?!"

"Most likely."

"OK, ohhhhh 'bearded Holmes,' then why the shoe theft?"

"Interesting you should ask. All criminals make mistakes. My guess, our Chinese *ring,*" with an edge to *ring,* "had a timetable. If I were making a bet I'd say the shoe thievery was the last of the effort by the *ring.* The flight out of town had already been bought and the *ring* ran out of time buying things for the shipwreck. The *ring* needed shoes so they just stole them all at once rather than buying them a few pair at a time. The *ring* didn't care about the investigation of the shoe theft because the ringleader would be long gone before there was a wrap-up."

"Well," Harriett tapped the folded paper against Noonan's desk. "According to this story, the perpetrators have fled the country."

"Isn't that wonderful," Noonan smiled. "Case closed."

Harriett smiled sardonically. "Not for the record, just the two of us. What tipped you this was an insurance scam?"

"The stuffed alligator. It would float. So would everything else. Ergo, whatever was planned had to do with water. It would be debris. Then I just called the six different marinas on the Tar River."

"Why the Tar River?"

Noonan broke into song:

Way down in North Car'lina,
On the banks of the Ole Tar River,
I go from there to Alabama,
For to see my ole Aunt Hannah.

Now Nancy, I must leave you,
Do not let our parting grieve you,
Dance and sing, forget your sorrow,
I'll be back sometime tomorrow.

THE MATTER OF THE
MISSING PTERIPPUS

Captain Noonan, the "Bearded Holmes" of the Sandersonville Police Department, was in a dodging conversation with his Administrative Assistant, Harriett. She was trying to convince him to take a call from the Sandersonville Commissioner for Homeland Security on Line 3 while Noonan was swearing he was not even in the office. He was, he declared, somewhere unreachable even by the electronic tool of Satan which he was required to carry with him at all times by the two people who could make such a demand, the Commissioner and a higher authority: his own wife.

He was knee-deep in the conversation swamp and losing when a blessed interlude was offered: Lt. Weasel. The officer blundered into the discussion by announcing "someone on Line 1 is looking for the 'Bearded Holmes.' He's missing some flying horses."

SAVED was the look on Noonan's face.

Harriett just rolled her eyes.

Before she was out of the room, Noonan was on Line 1. "Horses? Flying horses? That's rather odd. I didn't know horses could fly. There are horseflies of course, but they are not really horses."

"I've heard that before," the voice boomed over the phone line. "But I'm serious. I'm missing two flying horses."

"Really? And to whom am I speaking?"

"Jerome Jameson. Just like the liquor but I'm a teetotaler. I run the Sandersonville Carousel Company. Two night ago someone broke into the carousel warehouse and stole two of our flying horses. Why just the horses?"

Noonan dug through is desk to find his notebook. "Just the horses?"

"*Flying* horses." Jameson emphasized the word *flying*. "We've got lots of regular horses. On the carousel and in the warehouse. But what was stolen were the flying horses. The *pterippus*."

"I didn't catch that term," Noonan said as he struggled to write what he heard. "I thought flying horses were called Pegasus."

"A common mistake," Jamison said. "Pegasus is the name of one horse. The breed of horses, so to speak, who fly are *pterippus*. It's from the Greek: *pteros meaning winged and hippos for horse.*"

"I can live with that. Now, back to the stolen horses. You saw they were stolen off the carousel?"

"One was. The other was out of the warehouse."

"I am assuming there is a value to each of the *pterippus*?"

"I'm glad you used the correct term. Yes, but not a number you can put on a spread sheet. Our carousel is from the 1890s so the *pterippus* are priceless. We cannot replace them. We can buy replicas, of course, but that would sully our reputation. We pride ourselves as being unchanged over more than a century."

"Could the thief have stolen other figures from the carousel?"

"Of course. But there was something odd about the theft. The *pterippus* are unique. There are not many of them. We can find other animal figures from the 1890s. They are not exactly a dime a dozen but they are available on the market. They are just expensive. But the *pterippus* are unique so there are none on the market. So we want the *pterippus* back."

Horses, flying or otherwise, were new to Noonan. Never a horse man himself, his entire experience with horses – all three of them – were three rides on the same horse in summer camp in the last century. And that horse had been alive. Wooden horses who flew were a different breed of cat, so to speak.

But a crime was involved so to the computer he went. Had any other flying wooden horses been stolen? If so, when? Where? Was there a connection?

He got zip.

Then he tried carousels, merry-go-rounds and amusement park entries. Now he was overwhelmed. Every manner of crime associated with a circus, hippodrome, festival and fair – local, county, state and industrial – popped up. From failure to pay for popcorn to animal kidnapping was included. Animal kidnapping? It turned out to be a PETA 'attempt' to draw attention the inhumanity of cage animals. Inhumanity of caged *animals?* Noonan found that odd. He was in favor of caged felons so he didn't consider the caging of animals as being *inhumane*.

Only one crime seemed to be relevant to the theft of the two *pterippus*. "That was the way to pronounce it, right?" he mumbled to himself as he checked his notes. Then he made the call to a cell number. It was 775 area code, Reno, but with cell phones there was no way of knowing where the recipient of the phone call might actually be.

He was correct.

Sandra Wisconsin answered the call on her Beelzebubian electronic tool.

She was in Phoenix.

"A Wisconsin in Arizona," Noonan said after he identified himself. "How unusual."

"Could be." Wisconsin responded. "Did you find my carousel horses?"

A distant bell clanged in the recess of Noonan's brain.

"No. That's why I'm calling you."

"You're not with the Reno Police?"

"No. I'm calling from North Carolina. The Outer Banks. Do you know where they are?"

"Yeah. You've got the Spanish horses. The small ones. Shipwreck survivors. I know my animal history. Why are you calling me?"

"There was a theft of *pterippus* here . . ."

She cut him off. "Congratulations! Someone in law enforcement who knows the correct term! I'm impressed."

"Thanks. About your theft, what was stolen?"

"The whole kit and caboodle. While we were on hiatus, someone broke into our warehouse and stole all the animals.

We got them all back. If you read the police report you'd know that."

"Actually, I haven't read the report. You got all your animals back?"

"Yeah. They were found in a vacant lot about ten miles from the warehouse. They were all wet from the rain but we got them all back."

"None missing?"

"Nope."

"Did you have any *pterippus*?"

"Two. The usual for replica carousel."

Clang!

"Replica? So your carousel is not an antique?"

"Oh, no. I couldn't afford that. Besides, carousels take a beating. You wouldn't want to put something valuable like an antique figure out for the public to kick around."

"Your theft. Any idea why someone would steal the animals?"

"No. Like I said, I have replicas not original. I'm assuming the thieves thought our figures were antiques. Valuable. They are not."

"Couldn't they tell the figures were not antiques just by looking at them? I'm guessing your figures are made of plastic as opposed to wood."

"Right. You'd think so. But they stole the figures anyway."

"No damage of any of the figures?"

"A lot of scuffs and scrapes but I don't know if they were from the theft or the kids who ride the figures. The only damage I could not attribute to the kids was on the *pterippus*. There was some scarring on the bellies. Kids don't kick there."

Clang.

51

"What kind of scars?"

"Like someone was trying to split them open. My guess: they thought the *pterippus* were wood and would crack open like an egg. When they discovered the *pterippus* were plastic, they stopped."

"Any idea why?"

"No. But if it's important why don't you talk to Dave Gray at the Nevada Carousel Museum in Antioch. He's a storehouse of carousel trivia and history."

"You have a number for him?"

"Sure."

Dave Gray was more than pleased to hear from Noonan. Particularly after he used the term *pterippus.*

"I am so pleased when anyone uses that term," Gray told Noonan. "Did you know most cultures have flying horses?"

"No, I didn't."

"Different names, of course. There's Pegasus from the Greeks, *Al-Buraq* carried the prophet Muhammad, the Chinese have *Tianma* and *Chollima*. The Turks have *Tulpar* and in India, *Ucchisrava*s is created from the churning of oceans of milk."

"Interesting," Noonan said. "But I'm interested in antique wooden *pterippus.*"

"Historically, there are only two of the antique flying horse carousels still in existence. As far as I know. They are both called 'flying horse' carousels and both were constructed by Charles Dare. In 1876. One is in Oak Bluff, Massachusetts. It was originally at Coney Island but was moved to Oak Bluff to keep it from being sold piece-by-piece. It's owned by Martha's Vineyard Preservation Trust. The other one is in Watch Hill, Westerly, Rhode Island. Both of them have the flying horses.

They fly because the winged horses are on cables rather than attached to the flooring of the carousel. So, when the carousel rotates, the horses go up and down. Flying so to speak."

"Interesting," Noonan said. "Is there anything particularly valuable about the antique flying horses other than being antiques?"

There was a long moment of silence. Finally Gray said, "Not again! I thought we solved that problem?"

"What problem is that?" Noonan asked.

"It's an odd story. You said you were with the police?"

"In Sandersonville, North Carolina. We've had a theft of two winged horses. I take it this has happened before?"

"Oh, yeah," said Gray tiredly. "Yeah, yeah, yeah. Every dozen years or so. I call it the 'Search for Salvador's Millions.'"

"I'm all ears."

"You and Perot. Let's see. I'd say back in the late 1920s, just before the Great Depression, Charles 'Carousel Charlie' Salvador started this rumor he had secreted a million dollars in gold in one of the two winged horses he had. It was a publicity gimmick. You know, 'ride the million-dollar horse.'"

"Did the publicity work?"

"Who knows? It was in the 1920s and everyone had money."

"What happened to his winged horses?"

"Long gone. But over the years there have been thefts of winged horses with people looking for the gold. Every decade or so, winged horses get stolen and opened up. There never was any gold and most of the horses are just belly-damaged once the thieves realize the *pterippus* are solid wood."

"But the thefts continue."

"Yeah. But only idiots think there's gold in the winged horses. Think about. A million dollars in gold in the 1920s – or today – is on the order of 100 pounds. The minute anyone picks up a winged horse they have to know there is no gold inside."

"But the thefts keep coming?"

"You got it. What's the latest?"

"Two horses in Sandersonville."

"North Carolina, right?"

"That's correct."

"Sorry. Apparently you have some idiots out there."

"'fraid so. Does the carousel industry have any kind of a publication?"

"You mean like a magazine? Yes. I edit it."

"I have an idea. Will you save me some space in your next issue?"

"If it will stop idiots from stealing winged horse, of course."

Six weeks later Noonan was sitting in his office when his Administrative Assistant, Harriet, came in with a brick. It was covered with gold paint but there was clearly a brick beneath the paint.

"Ah," Noonan said when he saw the brick, "'Salvador's millions!' From Antioch, Nevada, no doubt."

"'Looks like a brick to me," sniped Harriet. "And I am a gal who knows gold when she sees it." She gave the brick a heft. "And this weighs like a brick, not gold."

"It's all in your mind, Harriett. To some this is a brick," he pointed to her with his coffee cup. "But to others, it is what dreams are made of," he said in a low growl.

"That's from the MALTESE FALCON. Even I know that."

"That," Noonan said continuing to point at the brick with his coffee cup, "is a crime solver. The thieves who stole those winged horses were looking for it."

"This?" Harriet looked at the brick with disdain. "Why?"

"They thought there was a 100 pounds of gold in the winged horses they stole. Sorry. No gold. So when they think that the gold," he pointed to the brick, "has been discovered in another winged horse, there was no reason to keep the horses they had."

"Ah," said Harriet. "Those were the two wooded horses we picked up at the beach last week?"

"Yes sire-e bobcat. When the *Nevada Carousel Magazine* announced the finding of 'Salvador's millions,'" he pointed at the brick, "that made the stolen horses worthless. So they were dumped."

"But aren't you clever. You salted a story and solved the crime. C-l-e-v-e-r." She hugged the brick to her chest. "So this is part of 'Salvador's millions.' My, my. You cannot accept gratuities so I will take these millions off your hands." She turned to go.

"Don't spend it all in the same place," Noonan said to her back as she left his office.

"I've got the perfect place for it." She replied over her shoulder.

"Really? Where?"

"Wall-mart."

THE MATTER OF THE ALLODIAL
SOCIALIST

Captain Noonan, the "Bearded Holmes" of the Sandersonville Police Department, was working his way through the Sunday *Sandersonville Chronicle*, an underground publication which had absolutely no socially redeeming articles save the Darwin Award nominees of the week garnered from news stories from around the world.

Then his phone rang.

At first, he was loath to answer the beast, primarily because it was mid-morning on a Tuesday and, technically, he was on annual leave. It was a use-it-or-lose-it situation and the only upside was his wife was out shopping and their twin sons were in school which left him the whole day by himself at home in blessed silence where he could concentrate on such important matters as who should make the top ten of the Darwin Awards this year, the Ugandan welder who blew himself and his neighborhood to pieces by soldering an empty gasoline storage tank from the inside – while wearing a gas mask to protect himself from the gasoline fumes still in the tank – or the California yuppie on the 15th floor of a high rise who pulled his waterbed out onto a flimsy balcony and proceeded to take out the other 14 balconies on his way down to the sidewalk where the pile of balconies with yuppie on the top toppled onto the string of cars parked along the curb including a police van and an armored car. The yuppie survived, which meant he was a Darwin Awardee-to-be, but the police and bank employees spent the next eight hours picking up $30,000 worth of quarters that were an apron of silver before the stack of balconies. "No Quarter for Yuppies," the headline had proclaimed while the article noted that the yuppie had survived with only a broken nose "and his Rolex still intact and ticking."

But that left the phone.

Looking at the digital readout he groaned. The call was from his administrative assistant, Harriet.

"I'm not here all day," he said into the mouthpiece when he picked it up. "I have been swallowed by a giant alligator who will only be released on payment of a case of anchovies to be delivered at midnight at the corner of Third and Fourth."

"That's fine with me," said a strange male voice on the line. "I'm only calling to find out why anyone would steal a broken samurai sword from the Russo-Japanese War, a used apron, six plastic spoons and a jade dragon from a museum."

"That's a good question. A better question is 'Who is this?'"

"Jennifer Nixon. I own the Socialist Museum here in Sylvester City. Those items were stolen from the museum last week. When I talked to the local police they just laughed. They thought I was kidding."

"I get the strangest phone calls in America so I am pretty sure you are not kidding about the samurai sword, used apron, plastic

57

spoons and jade dragon. But a socialist who owns something. Now that's rich!"

"Yes, I know. I'm an embarrassment to my cadre here in Sylvester City. I own something. I inherited it from my parents who, let me quickly add, were embarrassed I was socialistic. But that was when I had no money. Now that I have money, well, socialism isn't as attractive as it used to be."

"You mean the museum is making money."

"It always has. My parents owned the building free and clear and I lived in the attic. I turned the building into a museum about ten years ago."

"Why a Socialist Museum?"

"Well it used to be the Sylvester Museum but everyone in town kept calling it the Socialist Museum because I was well known as a socialist so I changed the name."

"How many socialists are there in Sylvester City?"

"Three. Me, my daughter and the librarian at the Sylvester City Library."

"A socialist working for the government? That's rich."

"He's 25 and my daughter's boyfriend."

"Ahhh!"

"I'm a capitalist now. The museum is making money."

"What does your daughter think of that?"

"She's a capitalist too."

"Once you become allodial, all things are possible."

"Allodial?"

"It's a real estate term. It means you own the real estate free and clear. You are an allodial socialist, two mutually exclusive concepts. Now, let's talk about your problem."

"Allodial. Doesn't that make me a capitalist?"

"It makes you an American. Socialism got us the national highway system, Hoover Dam and every public library, national park and state university from sea to shining sea. Capitalism lets you buy your choice of wine, brand of shoes and where to spend your two weeks of vacation every year."

"Heck of a choice. I like them both."

"Welcome to the United States of America. Tell me about the robbery."

"It wasn't much of a robbery. Like I said before, all that was stolen was a broken samurai sword from the Russo-Japanese War, a used apron, six plastic spoons and a jade dragon."

"Do any of these items have a high-ticket value?"

"Nope. The samurai is pretty average. It was given to us by a Korean War veteran and I have no idea where he got it. We had it appraised years ago and then it was only worth a hundred dollars. The plastic apron and spoons are worth nothing and the jade dragon is a pendant, not a stand-alone sculpture. You can buy dragons like the one that was stolen on eBay for under ten bucks."

"I can see why the police laughed. Nothing else missing?

"Nothing else was missing."

"Did anything get moved around?"

"You mean like furniture?"

"Yes. Or display cases."

"Funny you should mention that. The case with the samurai and the dragon was moved out and back."

"Would the thief have had to have moved the case that much to get the samurai and jade dragon out?"

"No. The front of the cabinet opens outwards."

"But the case was moved?

"Yes."

"How much?"

"I can't really tell. I'd say it was moved out two or three feet and then back."

"What is under the case?

"Nothing."

"No trap door to the basement?

"Nope. Just floorboards."

"When did the theft occur?"

"Over the weekend."

"Anything important happen over the weekend in Sylvester City?"

"Yes, actually. It was a big weekend for us. It was the 200th anniversary of the founding of the city. We drew quite a crowd. Everyone who was anyone was in Sylvester City was at the parade. It lasted a good three hours. Then we have an open-air barbeque."

"You were at the event?"

"All day. I sponsored the barbeque."

"You? A socialist?"

"Giving to the people. You don't have to be a socialist to do that."

"You were there all day?"

"All three days. I had to set up on Friday, serve on Saturday and then clean-up on Sunday. I didn't know about the theft until Monday when I opened the museum."

"Any sign of break-in?"

"No. But then again the building is not that secure. This is Sylvester City, for God's sake."

Noonan thanked her and said he would be in touch. Then he called the Sylvester City Mayor's Office and asked to speak to the City Manager.

"Henriette Midgette."

"Are you any relation to the Outer Banks Midgettes?"

"All Midgettes are related. What can I do for you?"

Noonan identified himself and asked about the 200th Anniversary celebration. Had anything unusual happened?"

"We're a small town," said Midgette. "There's always a lot of bickering beforehand. Then, once plans are made, everyone is fine with the arrangements. No one wants people outside of Sylvester City to think we're a bunch of yokels."

"Anyone in particular a pain in the tulip patch?"

"Tulip patch! That's a good one. I've got to remember it. All Democrats are a pain in the tulip patch. That's because the Mayor is a Republican. Next election it could be the other way around."

"What's the big issue?"

"Development. It always is. Republicans want roads and businesses. Democrats want schools and parks."

"Any red-hot button issues now?"

"Pull tabs and legalizing marijuana are always red-hot items. Pull tabs are legal if you buy them at an authorized store. Marijuana is not legal but no one is being busted for it."

"Are either pull tabs or marijuana a big problem?"

"For the police, yeah. But no one is getting arrested if that's what you mean."

"Not really. Any new roads being planned? Maybe a casino being talked about?"

"Not in this town. The casino anyway. There's always a road in the works."

"Anything happening near the Socialist Museum?"

"Is that what this is all about? What a dump! Jennifer Nixon is all right but that museum should have gone the way of the dinosaur. It gives her something to do but really, a Socialist Museum?"

"She's not popular?"

"She's all right. It's the daughter and boyfriend that are wingy."

"Wingy?"

"Strange. Odd. Unusual. Always doing strange things."

"Like selling marijuana?"

"No. Strange things like operating a food wagon that sells stuff like reindeer steak sandwiches and tilapia *quesadillas*."

"Why is that unusual?"

"We're a meat and potato town. People around here don't know what a *quesadilla* is and they think Rudolph was butchered for the sausages."

"Are they making any money?"

"Who knows? Their expenses are low because they live in the basement of the museum and own the mobile truck."

"How old is Jennifer Nixon?"

"Oh, I'd say 50ish."

"How about the daughter?"

"Mid 20s. Like the boyfriend."

"Honest folk?"

"Never been caught so I guess so."

When Noonan talked to the Sylvester City Police Station, he got a laugh when he asked about the Socialist Museum. "Don't spend a lot of time on that robbery, hear?"

"Not much to talk about?"

"Weird, odd, unusual. Nothing taken but penny-ante stuff. Not a drug burglary for sure."

"You have drug problems in Sylvester City?"

"Opioids. Just like every other city in America. But no reason to steal from the Socialist museum. It's got nothing of value."

"Does anyone actually visit the museum?"

"No locals. Just tourists."

"Other than opioids any big crime problems in Sylvester City? Bank robberies? Jewelry store heists?"

"We're just small-town America. Last bank robbery was in 1955 and we don't have a jewelry store. Some of the stores have jewelry counters but not stores as such."

"Any big drug busts?"

"Not the way you city people mean it. We go after meth labs and chase the cocaine dealers out of town. We probably see a couple of kilos of marijuana every year but not enough to worry us. We're a pretty quiet town."

"The samurai or jade dragon ever show up?"

"The Great Socialist Museum Heist! No. We can't figure out why anyone would steal the samurai or jade dragon much less the paper bags."

"There were paper bags stolen as well?"

"Maybe. They were reported stolen and then Jennifer called and said she found them."

When Jennifer Nixon called to say there had not really been a crime to report, she surprised when Noonan told her the samurai was in the mobile food van.

"How on earth did you know that?"

"Logical. Your daughter and her boyfriend needed a something to attract customers. A chef cutting reindeer into steaks with a samurai would do it. The samurai is for show anyway. I'll bet they took the samurai over the weekend and just forgot to tell you. I'm betting they used it over the weekend during the celebration. Probably used the apron and spoons as well. The ones you thought was missing."

"How did you know?

"Let me guess. Your daughter and her boyfriend probably told you after you called me that when they pulled the samurai out of the case the jade dragon fell and broke into pieces."

"I was told you were psychic. You certainly are."

"So that solves your robbery, a theft that never occurred."

"Everything's back to normal."

"Your daughter around?"

"Yes. Do you want to speak with her?"

"Yes."

When the daughter, Celeste, got on the phone Noonan asked how old she was.

"Why?"

"I just want to make sure you are old enough to understand me."

"What do you mean by that?"

"You know," continued Noonan. "I pulled up jade dragons on eBay and found they came in all sizes."

"So."

"And weights."

There was a long moment of silence. Finally Celeste said "So?"

"Well," said Noonan. "That jade dragon would be perfect as a counter weight for a scale. It doesn't look like something that would be used a counterweight. You could use it in a food wagon to precisely weigh something. Then you could sell that something in a paper bag. From the outside no one would know that one paper bag had a reindeer sandwich and the other had something else."

Again the long moment of silence.

Noonan continued. "If you can't make a living selling food out of a wagon, it's time to get into another line of business. I'm told Sylvester City has a fine community college, the first step toward a college degree in education. Who knows, someday you might inherit a museum."

THE MATTER OF THE ANCHOVY PIRATES OF THE BUXTON REEF

Captain Noonan, the "Bearded Holmes" of the Sandersonville Police Department, was deeply and personally involved with an anchovy, scallion and blue cheese sandwich, a pleasure only possible when his wife and twin sons were not within smelling – and thus – complaining distance. Not only did such a sandwich provide sustenance to the detective but it also brought back memories of his college years when he survived on such fare. Though he received a social science degree, he had attended an agricultural school where it possible for the less-than-affluent students to purloin agricultural products to supplement their meager educational stipends. The scallions could be uprooted from the experimental fields around the college and blue cheese, a subject of a dissertation by some unknown pre-professor, was in plentiful supply – if one had a friend who worked in the 'cheese laboratory' as it was called. Young Heinz Noonan, as a matter of fact but no historical record, did indeed have such a friend and dined on blue cheese frequently until the dissertation was completed.

The anchovies were another chapter of his life. Both his father and mother had treated anchovies as the food of the devil and were more inclined to consume lye with limburger cheese. Later, when he worked in a mom-and-pop pizza parlor, the young Noonan came to despise the solid, roasted anchovy spikes that were associated with cheap pizzas. It was only after his first Caesar salad did he truly come to appreciate the epicurean delight of the fillet. When he discovered the taste to which he was drawn was the noble anchovy, he was shocked. He had mistakenly believed anchovies only came in one form and that form was reflected in the spikes he had so infrequently sprinkled on pizza. The scales had fallen from his eyes.

Anchovies, as it happened, were an unexpected blessing in Buxton. Whenever he traveled south from Sandersonville to visit his wife's sisters' brothers, sisters and associated in-laws, outlaws, kith and kin, he made a point of visiting the surly men who fished for the anchovies on the notorious Buxton Reef. The Buxton Reef had originally been named the 'Jaws of the Deep' because of the abrupt manner which the coral upwelling rose from the bottom 100 feet down. The top of the reef, barely three feet from the surface of the brine, was just low enough that it was invisible from the surface of the water. More than a few ships have discovered the reef only when they were upon it. The early survivors of such wrecks became Buxton residents and thereafter land pirates profiting from the cargo that floated ashore after every subsequent wreck. The reef was locally known as and often called "Land Pirate Paradise" but that all changed when the amount of cargo coming ashore was greatly reduced by GPS and the United States Coast Guard. Fortunately for the Buxtonites, just as the booty from wreck ships went into decline, the invasion of the summer people began. Within a decade after the Second World War, the hamlet was making more off T-shirts, cheap meals and geegaws than on saltwater-soaked cargo. As sport fishing around the reef increased by a pleasing economic factor, the locals did not want any cash-paying Yankee to feel his/her life was in danger at the reef so, as in all things of a pecuniary nature, the colorful term for the reef changed to the mundane. It was now the Buxton Reef and all reference to its previous name was expunged from the public record.

However, there was one thing that the change of name, GPS and sport fishing industry could not expunge. That was the odd attraction of the reef to a unique species of fish: the Buxton anchovy: *Anchoa Buxtonoa*. This was an odd species, however. Though its size and color was similar to anchovies from other parts of the globe, it had a unique flavor because its diet was highly localized. Because of the reef's unique location, the upwelling brought localized Atlantic diatoms which are food of phytoplankton on which the anchovy feed. A different food source produces a different tasting anchovy and that was the unexpected charm of the Buxton anchovy.

But there was a problem.

Because the Buxton anchovy only existed in a single, confined location, it was constantly in danger of being placed on the endangered species list. This had more to do with the enthusiasm of a national environmental lobby which used the allegedly precarious state of the Buxton anchovy as a fund raising mechanism in Yankee cities where the environmentally-sensitive population was as large as it was uniformed. The Buxton Anchovy Pirates, self-named because the name poked fun at the same environmental lobby discussed in previous sentences, scoffed at the prospect they were over-fishing the resource. Permission to fish for anchovies was limited to a dozen ships and such ships were only allowed to cast their nets in the shallow water on alternating Tuesdays and Wednesdays from Memorial Day and Labor Day. Weekends, which in Buxton during that time period are Friday through Monday because of the summer people, were excluded because of the sport fishing crowd.

Perhaps the most expensive problem faced by the Buxton Anchovy Pirates was the shallow water of the reef. It took an experienced net hauler to reap the rewards of the reef and not snag the net on the coral. Nets were expensive so only the most seasoned of salts could operate the pulley and winch system.

It was one of these salts who approach Chief of Detectives Heinz Noonan with a unique problem while Noonan was dining on his celebrated sandwich.

"I see you're eating a fine sandwich, Professor." (The Pirates collectively referred to Noonan as 'Professor' because he was the only law enforcement official on the East Coast to whom they would speak without preceding and proceeding such with a heart-stopping profanity.)

"Another fine example of Buxton's best," Noonan replied to the old salt. "It's Wednesday and you're not fishing. I'm guessing you have a problem."

"You're right, Professor. We had a little bit of problem yesterday and all the boys said we should go to you first. We can't pay much for your services though, seeing what the shelf price of anchovies has been lately."

"I'll take my fee in anchovies. What's the problem?"

"It's odd."

"They all are."

"Well, we pulled up a figurehead in yesterday's net. It's from an old ship, has to be. It had barnacles and starfish all over it."

"That's a problem?"

"Not the masthead. The problem is what was attached to it: a ten-foot cable with a black box on it."

"A black box?"

"Actually the box is orange. It's one of those black box things that you see the President has. Like it has nuclear buttons in it. That kind of thing."

"What makes you think it's a black box?"

"Because on the side of it are the words: PROPERTY OF THE NORTH CAROLINA COMMISSIONER OF HOMELAND SECURITY, OPENING WITHOUT THE PROPER CODE SEQUENCE WILL RESULT IN AN EXPLOSION."

An hour later Noonan was at an anchovy warehouse looking over the catch of the day. What the pirate had asserted was true. The masthead had indeed been in the water for a substantial period of time, the proof being the encrustation of all manner of barnacles and other such assorted marine life which the detective recognized as such. The cable was old in the sense it was rusted. One end was secured around the masthead and buried in the encrustation. The other was looped numerous times around an orange container and secured with a padlock. And, as the pirate had also asserted, the wording on the side of the container had been accurately communicated.

Noonan took one look at the package and asked the simple question, "What's the problem? Call the North Carolina Commissioner of Homeland Security and have him come and pick up the box."

"Well," replied one of the pirates. "First off the Commissioner is a she, Gloria MacIntosh Houghton Sandoval. She's a hard core evangelical environmentalist. Five minutes after we turn the box over to her, the national newspaper would be running stories about Land Pirate Paradise. The anchovies would be on the endangered species list before the newspaper print was dry. We don't need that kind of publicity."

"You think the environmentalists are behind this?"

"Sure do. Who else?"

There was general agreement on both of these points from all the pirates. One of the younger men spoke, a young salt not yet seasoned, "We think they wanted the tide to drag the black box over the reef. It gets caught, blows open. The masthead floats away. Even if the masthead is found, there would have been no way to link the old masthead with the modern day black box. But an investigation is going to come up with pieces of that black box, all that orange metal on the dark reef is going to be easy to find and photograph. Suddenly it's a national security issue. That's how Homeland Security works."

"But why would they do that?"

"Because," said old salt, "Gloria MacIntosh Houghton Sandoval will use the excuse to put the Buxton anchovy on the endangered species list. Makes her look good to the environmental lobby. She's got a unique double political base you could only have in North Carolina: far right and far left. She gets the Buxton anchovy on the endangered species list; she can run for Governor. With her right wing credentials she'd look really good for a Republican Vice Presidential candidate."

"So you want me to make this problem go away? Is that what I'm hearing?"

"Well," said the old salt, "in a word, yeah . . . and we'll have to pay in anchovies."

"That's music to my ears." Noonan thought for a moment. "OK. Now I need you to do some things for me. I need you to ask casually – and I mean casually – up and down the coast to see where someone could buy an old masthead. That masthead is the key. It had to come from somewhere. Don't say a word about that black box. If word leaks out you'll have Homeland Security goons down here by the Winnebago-load; and I know how you like federal law enforcement people . . ." Noonan let the sentence hang.

There was general shuffling of feet, a lot of spitting and a chorus of unpleasant expletives.

"Now, what do you know about this Sandoval woman?"

"Gloria MacIntosh Houghton Sandoval," said the old salt. "She demands the whole name."

"And every one of those names is a rich environmentalist," snapped a young salt.

Noonan thought for a moment. "Not a lot of help there, eh?"

"Good bet," said the young salt.

"Well," said Noonan, "you find out about the masthead and I'll see what I can do for you."

The next day Noonan headed north for the main office of the Outer Banks National Environmental Protection Alliance in Scarborough. After he located the office he continued north to the first tourist shop on the outskirts of the community. There he bought a pair of shorts with an embroidered Hatteras lighthouse and a T-shirt that read "I © the Outer Banks." He removed his city clothes in the changing room and put on the shorts and T-shirt. They bought a pair of outlandish sunglasses, a floppy sun hat and some flip flops. Finally he purchased an OBX bumper sticker. Outside, he slapped the OBX on the front of his car – a rental and an action that was probably going to upset someone up the administrative food chain at the rental agency. Then he headed south.

Pulling up outside the Environmental Protection Alliance, Noonan parked his car right in front of the main window making certain the OBX bumper sticker was clearly visible to the man at the front desk who was, as is usually the case with environmental groups, the only paid person in the office.

Noonan opened the door with a huge OBEPA stenciled on the glass feeling a bit ridiculous dressed like a tourist considering he was a bona fide link to the founding families of Buxton. But dissembling was necessary so Noonan felt comfortable in his disguise.

Passing himself off as a tourist, a ruse his disguise was superb in supplementing, he said he wanted to make a donation to the "people who are preserving the exquisite natural environment of the Outer Banks." Then he wrote them a check for $1,000 which, his accountant had already assured him, was a legitimate charity deduction.

The environmentalist, a pleasant idealist by the name of Harrison Hamilton, was overjoyed at the donation.

"We can use all the help we can get," Hamilton said as he accepted the check. "Saving the Outer Banks from excessive development is going to be an expensive, lengthy process."

"I couldn't agree more," replied Noonan as he fiddled with the sun glasses that were irritating the tops of his ears. "There seems to be a lot of development, particularly around Buxton. How is the development affecting the fish?"

Hamilton thought for a moment. "Kind of depends on the fish you're talking about. A lot of the sports fish are so far out they aren't affected by the land development. The real problem is the fouling of estuarine waters in the near shore area, particularly on the Pamlico Sound side. The power of Atlantic storms keeps people from building too close to the water on the east side. But you can build right to the water's edge on the other side. That's where the problem is going to be."

"That's too bad," Noonan noted with a sad tone, partly to stay consistent with his disguise and partly because he had many relatives with Pamlico Sound side property. But, being there on duty so to speak, he pressed the issue of the anchovy pirates. "So there's no problem with the Atlantic-side fish?"

"Well, there's the usual," said Hamilton. "There's a lot of over-fishing because of the increase in tourism. However the fish populations have proven to be very resilient. We think that's because of the incredible upwelling of food. That's why we have anchovies."

"Anchovies?" Noonan clearly hoped he sounded surprised. "I didn't know there were anchovies in this part of the ocean."

"There's a small fishery of them out on the reef. But they are far enough off shore that they are not being affected by shore pollution. There's plenty of upwelling out there so the population is strong. We're also fortunate there are anchovy fishermen."

"Really, why's that?"

"Well, anchovies come in schools so there has to be a lot of food to keep the schools full. Under natural conditions a school will grow to as large as its available food supply. The big problem with schools of fish, particularly in unique areas like the Buxton Reef, is they are in such a confined area they devour all available food. No excess food means no other species. But in the case of the Buxton Reef, the anchovy fishermen have been keeping the schools smaller than their food supply. Over an extended period of time, a lot of sport fish moved into the area. We've got a real ecological/economic success story out there. The anchovy fisherman are making a living, the sport fishing boats are making a living, the anchovy stock is not declining and the sport fish population is rebounding after each season. It's one of our unpublicized success stories."

"That's interesting," Noonan said. "So the anchovy fishermen are actually doing the environment a service?"

"Absolutely! If they stopped fishing, the anchovy schools would jump in size and eat the other species out of the area. In about two years there wouldn't be a bite of food for any other species of fish. That would devastate the sport fishing industry in Buxton, Avon, Scarborough and Hatteras. So, yeah, those anchovy fishermen are doing the environment a heck of a favor."

It took the anchovy pirates less time to find the source of the masthead.

"Them bastards," said the old salt when he spotted Noonan getting out of his car at his sister-in-law's brother's brother's home. "Professor," said the wizened pirate as he tapped a calloused finger on Noonan's chest, "you look like a tourist!"

"Disguise, George. It's a disguise. Who are the bastards?"

"Homeland Security. They bought the masthead."

"How do you know that?"

"Easy, Professor. There was only one place you could find anything like that, in the boat graveyard in the Scarborough

Slough. That's Old Man Russel's place; he's my sister's brother-in-law."

"Is everyone down here related to everyone else?"

"Everyone but the Coasties."

"Yeah. About Old Man Russel?"

"We don't get along *at all* but we have a close friend in common, John Walker. After some socializing he said he gave the masthead to a federal agency he could not name. He didn't charge them because they said it was in the interest of national security."

"You sure it was the Office of Homeland Security?"

"Well, Old Man Russel hates the Coast Guard, wouldn't give the FBI a bad habit, is convinced the CIA is listening to his brainwaves through his dental plates, has three accountants just to confuse the IRS, thinks United States Marshals are children of Darth Vader and is related to every law enforcement official on the Outer Banks. Do I think it was Homeland Security? Old Man Russel is so cheap he wouldn't give his grandmother a dime if she starving to death. But if someone said it was for national security, he'd give them the farm. Yeah, it was Homeland Security."

"Well, that narrows the field. By the way, the environmentalists think you're doing a great job by catching anchovies. By the way."

"Nahhhhhh."

"Yeahhhhhhhhh."

Gloria MacIntosh Houghton Sandoval looked exactly as Noonan had expected she would look: an elegant mix of WASP and Mediterranean stock. Her hair was blond, probably colored considering her ethnic stock. Her nails were perfectly manicured and her Ralph Lauren suit was perfect for her slender frame. She sat behind an expensive mahogany desk and fiddled with a letter opener as Noonan sat down in the oversized leather chair, framed by a portrait of her family on one forward corner of her desk and a wooden crucifix on the other.

Noonan, for his part, was dressed just the way he expected she would expect him to dress. In uniform. It was the first time he had worn his uniform in more than a year and the previous time had been a charity benefit. Sandersonville had not had an officer die in the line of duty since the end of the Civil War so Noonan's uniform was only brought out on special occasions – and he hated every one of those occasions.

Except this one.

To mollify his displeasure at having to wear his uniform, he considered it a disguise for undercover work. Odd, he thought, how he could be wearing his uniform in public yet it was a disguise for undercover work.

"Commissioner Lizzard gives you high marks for solving crimes and other matters," Sandoval smiled like the politician she was. "What, exactly, are 'other matters?'"

Noonan smiled, again, part of his disguise. "Well, I guess you'd say a lot of matters come up that aren't crimes but they still have to be resolved. As an example, I was once called upon to determine why a corpse was making obscene phone calls."

Sandoval was surprised. "I find it hard to believe a corpse would be making any kind of phone calls."

"I felt the same way. But someone was making those calls. My job was to stop the calls."

"Did you?"

"Yes, but it's a long story."

"One of these days when you and I have more time, I'd like to hear that one. But, as you know, our nation's security is at risk every moment of every day. So what can I do for the Sandersonville Police Department?"

"Actually, it's more in line with what we can do for you. We've stumbled on a situation we really should pass on to the government but there isn't an office that fits, if you know what I mean."

"Actually, I don't."

"Last week, we got a tip on a sale of government computer hard drives. We aren't sure why anyone would want to buy old government hard drives but someone was selling them. We checked and found an entrepreneur had purchased the hard drives legitimately. From a federal surplus property division. We checked to make sure the sale was legitimate and spent a couple of hours looking at the paperwork to make sure there were no law enforcement or Department of Defense hard drives in the bunch."

"Good precaution."

"We did find one from Fish and Wildlife and since they have a law enforcement arm, we asked to search it ourselves – just in case, you know."

Sandoval went from slightly condescending to a bit more than interested. "Did you find anything?"

"Yes and no. There were no law enforcement files on the drive and what was left had been almost completely wiped clean, I guess that's the term."

"Something was left?" Sandoval's interest blossoming.

"Sort of. Half-and-half if you know what I mean. A memo or file or something like that. A computer is black magic to me. Our IT tech said the file was probably on the desk top so it wasn't erased when the files were. Then the hard drive was scrubbed again and most of the memo or file was erased. What was left was a jumble of words, half letters and the like on bands of lines. It wasn't totally readable. Of what we could read it appeared to us to be a discussion of a rumor that someone was buying 'marine artifacts' as 'flotation devices.' Those words were clear. One word that we pieced together seemed to read 'explosive,' 'explosion,' or 'explodes' and in the next line were letters which might have formed the word 'black box.' To us that is a catchphrase for some kind of command and control device like the President has or a plane has in its cockpit. We don't see how they can be explosive so we don't know what we have."

Sandoval casually ran her right index finger across his right eyebrow. "Did you contact anyone to see if they could give you more information?"

"We were able to trace the hard drive back to Fish and Wildlife but that was as far as it went. No staff person had a specifically assigned computer so that hard drive could have been used by anyone – or lots of any ones – or, for that matter, a member of the public. No one knew anything about a black box. They said *marine artifact* was probably something like the piece of a shipwreck or what came off a wrecked ship. Their definition of a *floatation device* was the same as mine. They don't deal with explosives so they couldn't help me beyond that."

"So what do you think is going on?" Sandoval was now edgy.

"We're not sure. Our gut feeling is someone is setting the government up for a big law suit. A perp puts an explosive device on something that looks like a pieces of a shipwreck.

The perp then pulls the pieces of shipwreck with the explosive next to his ship and the device explodes. The black box will be found on or near the wreck so the perp can claim the military sank his ship by accident. There could be some pretty big bucks there because a black box is not something someone just loses."

Sandoval had now gone from highly interested to nervous. "What are you going to do about it?"

"Well," Noonan feigned concern, "we're going to be putting out an alert to all law enforcement agencies, marinas, docks and harbors around Pamlico and Albemarle sounds to be very careful of anything floating that looks like part of a shipwreck. That's a start. Then we'd like Homeland Security to casually inquire among federal law enforcement agencies and the Department of Defense to see if any black boxes are missing. No one is going to tell us if a black box is missing but they will tell you. If there is a black box missing we can find the perp by tracing its origin. That's going to be a lot easier than trying to find a marine artifact and trace its origin."

Sandoval slowly stood up and walked to the window in her office. She absentmindedly stroked her skirt.

"Humm," was all she said, indicating she was thinking that Noonan was to wait until she had formed her idea. She turned around, stared at the ceiling for a full minute and then sat down. "As you know, the President is very concerned about the welfare of all Americans when it comes to terrorism." She smiled. "I talk with him on a regular basis and one of the points he continues to drive home to all us in the field is that being vigilant does not mean to precipitate a panic. All we have here is a part of a memo that refers to a rumor you can't trace. For the moment, let's hold off on sending out any references to this alleged plot. Frankly, I don't believe any agency is missing a black box but I will check. If a black box is missing, we can get the alerts out. In the meantime, for the sake of the country and our President's war on terrorism, let's keep this little talk classified."

"I don't have any problem with that."

Two days later Noonan got a package at his office in Sandersonville. It had no return address but there was a Buxton stamp beside the address label. Inside he found a case of Buxton anchovy: *Anchoa Buxtonoa* with a handwritten note on top that read "More where these came from."

Harriet saw him and the anchovies and pinched her face up as if she'd been eating lemons. "You don't actually eat those, do you?"

"A find gourmet food, Harriet. A gift of Poseidon."

"Not for me. That's just another kind of sardine. You got a call, by the way. Someone who wouldn't leave his name and called you the 'Professor.'"

"Did he sound like he'd been drinking?"

"How'd you know that?"

"A good guess. What did he say?"

"I don't know for sure but I copied it down. 'The men in black picked up the box of orange and it went bang when it was dropped in the blue-and-white.' Does that mean anything to you?"

"It means that Homeland Security is on the job." He offered her a tin of anchovies. "Care for a flat?"

THE MATTER OF THE DROWNED MAN IN A HOT AIR BALLOON

Captain Noonan, the "Bearded Holmes" of the Sandersonville Police Department, was pondering a particularly difficult move on the cloth chessboard that hung on the wall of his office. His King was hiding behind the Knight's Pawn and he was trying to lure Captain Sandoval of the Miami Police Department, by phone, into a double attack. They made contact every few days and Noonan was waiting to spring a trap.

"That call you've been waiting for is on Line 3," Harriet, his administrative assistant and office common sense maven, said sullenly over the intercom.

"Yeah. Yeah," Noonan snapped as he picked up the receiver and punched Line 3. "Don't tell me. It's Queen to Bishop Seven, right?"

"No," came a female voice over the line. "It's a drowning in a hot air balloon. Do I have Captain Noonan?"

"Yes," Noonan said, trying to capture his thoughts. "This isn't Captain Sandoval of the Miami Police?"

"No. This is Lt. Harriet Hellenthal of the Mazatzal Police Department in Arizona."

"Arizona?"

"Yes, sir."

"Just a moment," muttered Noonan and put Lt. Hellenthal on hold. He buzzed Harriet.

"You told me I was expecting this call."

"I didn't say that. The Chief of Police did. That's why I patched her through."

"I was expecting a call from Captain Sandoval?"

"Oh, you got that one too. I've got a message."

"Yeah?"

"I don't understand it but it's 'Knight takes Rook. Ha. Ha.' Do you know what he means?"

"Yeah," said Noonan as he looked at the cloth chessboard despondently. Then he punched Line 3 again. "What can I do for you Lt. Hellenthal. It is Hellenthal, isn't it?"

"Yes, it is. Your name was given to me by the Chief of Police in Tucson. He said we had exactly the kind of a case you love to solve."

"I can't imagine what he was talking about."

"Well, I called the Commissioner of Homeland Security in Sandersonville and he seemed to agree."

"He would," said Noonan and he dragged the phone over to the cloth chessboard and replaced the black Rook with a white Knight. "What can I do for you?" he asked as he brought up the chess-by-mail program on his computer and logged the move.

"I'm with the Mazatzal Police Department. We're a small community of 150,000 about 100 miles northeast of Phoenix, on the far side of Horseshoe Reservoir.

"I imagine it's rather hot down there. What can I do for you?

"Yes, it is. 95 right now and it isn't noon yet. We have a very small law enforcement community here, 30 people including the meter maids, coroner, magistrate and patrolmen. We use the State of Arizona Crime Lab when we have a technical problem but this death falls under the category of unusual."

"Tell me about it."

"Well, three months ago we had a hot air balloon race that started at the far side of Horseshoe Reservoir and ended on the shore of Bartlett Reservoir near the community of Sunflower. It's pretty rugged country but we were going to do our chasing by boat."

"Chasing?"

"Right. Ballooning is done in pairs. One team rides in a balloon and the other has a truck on the ground. That way both teams meet when the balloon comes to ground."

"But for this race you were going to use boats on the reservoir?"

"Right. These balloonists were very experienced so traveling that far over water wasn't a problem. They would be high enough that if anything normal went wrong – not that anything goes wrong normally, if you know what I mean."

"Yes, quite. Please continue."

"One of the participants was a member of the police force, Sgt. Jane Williams. She was not a particularly well-liked individual but she did her job well."

"What happened to Sgt. Williams?"

"She was alive when she went aloft. Two hours later her balloon was spotted flying without a pilot. A fixed wing, er, . . .

"A plane."

"That's right. A plane was sent aloft but the pilot could not see anything. When the balloon finally approached where the desert began, the pilot shot a hole in the balloon with a shotgun. When the balloon landed we found Sgt. Williams dead."

"Uh, huh." Noonan was fiddling with a letter opener. "Something tells me there's more to this story."

"There is. According to the coroner, she drowned."

"Drowned as in she came down in the middle of the reservoir, drowned, and then the balloon took her away?"

"No, sir. The water in her lungs was salt water. The reservoir is fresh water. Her balloon left with everyone else's and no one saw her anywhere near the water."

"Now I see why the crime lab can't help you. How close is the nearest salt water?"

"372 miles. We had a law-and-order picnic on the shores of the Gulf of California in Mexico about six months ago. How far it was to the ocean was a lottery so we know it's exactly 372 miles."

"Did Sgt. Williams go on that trip?"

"No."

"Were there any cuts or bruises on the victim?"

"Quite a few of them. When the balloon came down it came down quite hard. It basically dropped like a stone from at least a 1,000 feet up."

"Any of them caused before death?"

"Very little way of knowing."

"No sign of a struggle, skin under fingernails, the usual?"

"No."

"If she was so badly battered, how did the coroner come to the conclusion she had died of drowning in salt water?"

"Because some was found in her lungs."

"Do you have any good suspects?"

"Not a one."

"You said that she was not well-liked. What did you mean by that?"

"She was a very selfish person, put herself ahead of others. No one trusted her. She's one of those people who got a job because she was a female in the days of Affirmative Action and hasn't learned anything since. She bolted from one of her partners while they were under fire and turned in another for alleged sexual harassment."

"Was the charge true?"

"No."

"So you'd have to say that she wasn't very popular with the rank and file."

"That's right. She couldn't be fired and no one could work with her."

"Was she married? Did she have family?"

"Her husband works in coroner's office. They have two children, 10 and 11, I think. Her father is retired but lives in town and her mother, now remarried, lives in Tucson. Her brother works for us in records and her sister and her husband work for the magistrate. She's got some other cousins or whatever. One of them is a patrolman and the other is a clerk."

"A big happy family. Was it a happy marriage?"

"Not really. She ran around a lot. She had a trapline of men but no one steady."

"Did her husband know it?"

"He does now."

"When did he find out?"

"As far as we can tell, he didn't know until the day we started the murder investigation."

"How about the boy friends? How many of them were at the start of the race?"

"All of them."

"And the husband?"

"He was there and most of the close relatives were too."

"Was the woman who got into the balloon in the morning at the start of the race positively identified as Sgt. Williams?"

"Yes. We all knew her."

"She was seen getting into the balloon?"

"Not really. She was seen the morning of the race. She was seen standing in the balloon basket at the start of the race. That was the last time anyone saw her alive."

"Did she wave to anyone from the balloon?"

"At the start of a race? Naw, that wasn't her style."

"What *was* her style?"

"She was known to drop her required ballast as soon as the rules allowed and then blast as high as possible as soon as possible. That's a risky proposition in a race."

"Why?"

"The person who will win a balloon race is the one who will cover the set distance in the shortest period of time. Usually that means going up slowly, finding a cross current and then riding it in the direction of the end of the race. If you rise too fast, like Sgt. Williams did, you run the risk of passing through cross currents without even feeling them."

"So when the race started she went, quite literally, straight up?"

"That's right. Dropped all her ballast at the start of the race and pulled the burn cord on the balloon straight down."

"Was her husband a balloonist? How about her boyfriends?"

"The husband was a spotter but rarely went up. He just supported her passion. As far as her boyfriends are concerned, I don't know."

"Could you find out?"

"For those boyfriends we've identified, yes."

"Could there have been anyone else in the balloon with her?"

"Not really. If there had been anyone else in the basket the balloon would have ridden sluggishly. As it was, she jumped into the sky. No. There wasn't anyone else in the basket."

"Was there anything unusual in the basket?"

"It was pretty badly broken up but the lab went over the basket thoroughly. There was nothing unusual we could find."

"Any extra holes? Trapdoors?"

"Nope."

"Was there anything at all that was unusual no matter how insignificant you may consider it?"

"She was legally drunk, but then we all were that morning."

"How drunk?"

"1.5. Like the rest of us."

"Was she a heavy drinker?"

"Not really. We were all drinking whiskey that morning. We didn't want to drink beer because . . ."

"I can imagine."

"Did you see her when the race started?"

"Not in the way you mean. All of the balloons were lined up and the pilots were inside the baskets. The gun sounded and we left. She shot straight up out of sight like she usually does and that's the end of the story."

"Where is her body now?"

"In the morgue."

"All right. I'll tell you what I'll do. I'll give it a day and roll some possibilities around in my mind. But I want you to do some checking for me."

"I've got my pencil and paper ready."

"I like your attitude. First, was the water in her lungs water with salt, ocean water, saltwater from an aquarium or water that just appeared to be salted? Second, did her husband, boyfriends or any of her family go on that law-and-order ocean trip? Third, who benefits financially from Sgt. Williams death and how much are we talking about? Fourth, fourth?, fourth? I can't think of a fourth so I guess the three I gave you will have to do."

"I'll do what I can. Should I call you at this number tomorrow about this time?"

Noonan looked longingly at the cloth chessboard on his wall. "Maybe a little later."

"Sorry?"

"Never mind. I'll talk to you tomorrow."

Noonan was still pondering his vulnerable first rank the next morning when Lt. Hellenthal called back.

"Lt. Hellenthal! I've been thinking about your problem all night! Did you get me the answers I needed?"

"Yes, but I don't know how much help they will be."

"Spill."

"OK. The best the coroner can tell, it was ocean water. It could have come from a salt water aquarium if it didn't use the usual pet shop chemicals. The husband of Sgt. Williams went on the law-and-order trip as did at least one of her boyfriends. He's a patrolman. But, like I said yesterday, we don't know all of her boyfriends so there could have been another one there as well. As far as her will is concerned, she leaves an estate of about $20,000 to her husband and children and her insurance leaves $100,000 to her children."

"Is there one of those double indemnity clauses?"

"Yes. But only if killed in the line of duty."

There was silence for a moment. When Noonan said nothing Lt. Hellenthal came back on the line.

"Captain Noonan? Are you still there?"

"Yes. Yes. I'm just thinking."

"Would you like me to call back?"

"No. No. Let's see. First, how she was killed. Actually it was quite simple. Whoever killed her did it on the ground in the basket of the balloon. There was no reason to be clever about it because he thought her body would never be found. If it was, as long as he used a blunt instrument he was going to escape detection. Any chemicals would have left a residue. It would have been easy because she was drunk and knew her killer. After she had been killed, a rope was looped around her right wrist. She was pulled erect by the rope and that's the position she was in when the gun went off to start the race. She only had to be visible erect for a few seconds. No one was near her or looking at her closely when the race started so there was no reason to suspect she was dead."

"But she had to be alive to go aloft."

"Not really. Her usual practice, as you told me, was to drop all her ballast at the beginning of the race and rise as high as possible and quickly as possible. When the gun went off, the killer had all of the ballast fall away from the balloon. The burner on the hot air balloon was probably jammed so it would leap into the sky."

"But you can't leave a burner on for very long or you'll burn out the bag. That means short bursts."

"The killer was planning on that. Remember, the race was over water. The killer figured she'd rise too fast and the bag would burn. Once the bag went, that would be the end of Sgt. Williams. The balloon would erupt into flames. Then she, the balloon and basket would fall into the reservoir. End of story. The rope that was looped on her wrist was probably run around the burner. When it got hot enough, it burned through. That way, if the balloon was ever found she wouldn't be discovered tied to the burner."

"But the coroner said she drowned!"

"That's what fooled everyone for so long. What probably happened was the burner on the balloon shut off. I'd guess there is some kind of automatic shut off mechanism to keep the balloon from burning. The killer didn't know that. He didn't know balloons that well. So there was his victim, up in the sky and sailing along. She was dead and when she came down it wouldn't take too long for the police to put two and two together. After all, I'm betting that there were photos of start of the race, maybe even some videos. The killer didn't know what was in those photos or on those videos. So he had to muddy the waters of the investigation."

"What you're saying is the salt water was a ploy by the coroner to cover up his own murder."

"Or by someone he knew and was covering up for. Or by someone in the coroner's office. Or by someone who was responsible for handling the body. Or by someone at the crime scene. That body had to be pretty badly broken after falling 1,000 feet. As soon as the balloon didn't fall out of the sky, the murder needed Plan B. But he had time, a few hours, right?"

"Yeah. She was in the air a few hours before she was shot down."

"Right. The murderer could have taken some salt water from an aquarium or, if he had been planning ahead, he might have collected some from the ocean on that law-and-order trip. He didn't need much, maybe as little as a syringe-full. The point was to make it *appear* as though she had drowned."

"I see. But wouldn't that have kept the case open rather than closing it?"

"No. It sent you off on a red herring. If it had been a normal investigation, you might have spotted the murder right away from the photos and video. Now, what, three months later the trail is pretty cold. If your murderer is smart he's seen every photo and foot of video taken at the start of the race. Any photos or footage that would incriminate him are probably now gone. Lost. Your murderer is still around, somewhere. He's a member of your law-and-order fraternity there."

"That's not a very pleasant thought."

"I can understand that. But if you really want to find the murderer, recheck all of the negatives of the photos taken at the start of the race. Compare those with the actual photographs that were collected for the investigation. If you find a photograph missing, that will tell you who your murder is."

"It's certainly worth a try. Thank you very much for your help. If there is anything we can every do for you, please let us know."

"Good. Good." Noonan's eyes drifted to the cloth chessboard on his wall. "Would you happen to know how to defend your first rank against an about-to-be discovered Check?"

"Why not ask an expert? Try Bobby Fischer."

Before Noonan could respond, the line went dead.

THE MATTER OF THE DRAINED LORRY

Heinz Noonan, the "Bearded Holmes" of the Sandersonville Police Department, was pleasantly and uncharacteristically jovial with Mary. He loved Mary. He enjoyed the company of Mary. Particularly when he was in Alaska because in Alaska he was on vacation – except when his mother-in-law was within talking distance. His wife, Lorelei, as luck would have it, was off with their twins on some Alaskan enterprise which was fine with Noonan because it left him alone with Mary. His favorite vacation companion. Mary. Bloody Mary. And all her kith and kin. Ah, yes, Mary was indeed the perfect vacation companion.

Mary continued to be the perfect vacation partner until Noonan's mother-in-law broke into his holiday repose with the tool of Satan. She handed him the electronic Lucifer and said, "It's some Japanese guy from Beaver."

Noonan grunted, which was his technique for ending conversations with his mother-in-law, and took the iPhone fiend with dissatisfaction but, with satisfaction, because he watched his mother-in-law leave the gazebo where he was ensconced. Only then did he answer the phone.

"Noonan here."

"Captain Noonan?"

"Not while I'm on vacation. Here it's Heinz."

"OK. Heinz. This is Jacob Asahi. I'm calling from Beaver. Up on the Yukon. I'm sure you've never . . ."

Noonan cut him off. "As a matter of historical fact, I do know where Beaver is and its unusual history. You clearly have a Japanese name so that fits with Beaver's history."

"I'm surprised, sir, er, Heinz."

"Don't be. If you know your Alaskan history you know all about Beaver. Founded by Japanese-Inupiat refugees from Barrow during the Second World War. The Japanese and their Inupiat relatives had a choice: move inland or go to relocation centers for the entire war in the Lower 48. They chose to move inland and founded Beaver."

"I'm impressed. Not that many Alaskans know about Beaver."

"It's all history, son. All history. I'll also bet you're a VPSO because I doubt Beaver is large enough to fund a State Trooper."

"Again, you are right. I am the VPSO and we have a population of a little more than 80. However, that does not keep crime at bay. We've got an odd problem here and you have a reputation of solving unusual crimes."

"Sometimes I can; other times, not so much. What's your 'odd problem?'"

"Someone's stealing water out of our water tank lorry."

Noonan, a veteran of decades of odd, weird and impossible crimes, was a bit taken aback. "Water. As in what you drink? I mean, Beaver, Alaska. That's on the Yukon, right? So, when it comes to water, I'm betting you have more than you fair share. That's quite a bit considering Los Angeles is running out of water. On top of that, a lorry is the English word for truck. Do I, at least, have that right?"

"Answering your questions backwards, yes, a lorry is the English word for truck. The man who started the water truck business here in Beaver had an English mother. He used a lot of English English, if you know what I mean. Ate odd things too, like kidney pie and blood pudding."

"Neither of those are on list of favorite foods," Noonan said blanching. "But you are on the Yukon River."

"Right on the bank of the river, yes. But that's river water. The water being taken, stolen, removed, whatever, was in a water tank truck, a lorry."

Noonan was having a hard time understanding what he was being told. "Let me see if I have this right. You live in a village on the banks of the Yukon River, one of the largest in the world, and someone is stealing water out of a tank truck?"

"Correct."

"I'm assuming the tank truck has filtered water, not water taken directly from the river."

"Yes and no."

"I hate answers like that."

"We have two tank trucks. One is for drinking water when it is needed out of town. We are a small village but we do have a small filtration plant. The drinking water lorry, er, truck is small, 750 gallons. The larger truck, 5,000 gallons, is for road work, construction projects and the like. It isn't used that often which is why we didn't know about the water thefts until recently. The smaller truck is used frequently."

"So the water being stolen is unfiltered."

"As far as we know."

"What do you mean by 'as far as we know?'"

There was a pause on the other end of the electronic line. "Well, we only know water has been stolen because of the mileage. We had to do an audit and found the mileage for the two trucks was way off. Off by several hundred miles. We have to record the miles for the record book but since we have several drivers, no one noticed the discrepancy. Drivers just logged in the start and finish mileage and that was that. They don't check to make sure the starting mileage is the same as the finishing mileage from the last driver. Or trip. But when we looked over the books, we found the trucks had been making extra trips. All were about 35 miles. That's 17 and half out and back. There's nothing special 17 and half miles out of Beaver so we don't know what's going on."

"What is 17 and a half miles out of Beaver?"

"Not much. Some beaver dams, what's left of a spill pile ridge from a dredge from 50 or 60 years ago, an airstrip from the Second World War, some decrepit World War II barracks that have been stripped of all boards, an old gold mine that went belly-up in the 1930s and some trap line cabins."

"Nothing of value?"

"Believe me, if there was anything of value out there someone in Beaver would have been on it like white on rice."

"That's an odd idiom to use for someone in Beaver."

"Maybe but everyone here is always looking for a way to make a buck. We're in the bush and money is hard to come by."

Noonan smiled as he shook his head. "Let me think. Here are some questions. I'm guessing whatever is happening is taking place 17 and half miles out of Beaver. So, in that location, how many beaver ponds are there, how big are they, how long and wide is the landing strip, when was the spoil pile ridge dropped, who actually owns the land under the abandoned barracks, who actually owns the old gold mine, is any of the land in the area part of a national forest or preserve, have there been any hints of a large company looking to come into Beaver and, I guess lastly, is anyone in town in deep debt."

"I can answer all of those questions. Do you want the answers now?"

"Shoot."

"OK. There are at least a dozen beaver ponds in the area, six or seven of them are on tributaries from the main river. The largest beaver pond is about the size of a small lake and it is the oldest. The spoil pile ridge is from a dredge that was abandoned about five miles upriver. Everything usable from the dredge is long gone. All that is left are the buckets and the skeleton of the ship. The last time the dredge was used was in my grandfather's day. The landing strips is about as wide as a football field and twice as long. It is still usable. That is, it is not overgrown and there are no large trees at either end. None of the land in that area has any special designation and anyone can start a mine or take over an old one. Or the barracks for that matter. All they have to do is file a claim. No big company is looking to come in and *everyone* in Beaver is deep in debt."

Noonan thought for a moment and then said. "Let me tell you what I think I know. When someone works a mine, they take out tons of debris to find ounces of gold. But when it comes to a dredge, the buckets pull up hundreds of pounds of soil from the bottom of a river and sieve out nuggets. The difference between the two is the mine can recover gold all way down to dust flakes while the dredge only gets large pieces of gold. The smaller sizes of gold, the flakes, get left behind by the dredge."

"Basically, yes. The very small bits of gold, the dust, are never really recoverable. They are so small it would cost more to recover them than they are worth. The big chunks of gold, the nuggets, were taken out of the mine and dredge piles years ago. You could pan the dredge spoil pile ridge for the gold that was left but we're talking about a five-mile-long snaking of earth and rock that's, say, ten feet high and 30 feet wide."

"But there is gold in the spoil pile?"

"Absolutely. About as much as was taken out by the dredge. But it's all small stuff, flakes. It would take a lot of work to dig through the overburden."

Noonan went silent for so long Asahi had to ask if he was still there.

"I'm still here. I'm not going to fly out to Beaver so I'll take a wild guess. If I had to bet I'd say whoever is stealing the water is dumping it into the beaver ponds. Why? Again my guess. If he can put enough water in the large pond, the old one you mentioned, it will break. Since there are no beavers in that pond, there will be no repair. The overflow will flood the other ponds one at a time and break them open. With luck – luck if you were the perp – there will be a flood of water over the spoil pile and a lot of the soil will wash away. That will reveal the gold in the spoil pile. It would be just like panning for gold expect the flooding water is doing the swirling. It would be like a long tom, if you know your Alaska Gold Rush history. The water will flood over the spoil pile until the beavers repaired the other dams. But between the time the old dam breaks and the beavers repair the newer ones, the flooding water will do the work of a small sluice. Why not set up one of those remote cameras near the old beaver dam. Maybe you can get a snapshot of the perp."

"I had not thought of that. Let me see what I can do."

Before Noonan could add a word, the satanic invention went, blessedly, silent.

A week later Noonan got a package.

From Beaver and it was the first time he had thought of Asahi and the drained lorry since the beast of Beelzebub had gone silent. Inside was a dark snapshot of a water truck – or lorry as Asahi called it – pumping water into a large lake. It had to be a beaver pond because Noonan could see stickwork near where the water was being dumped. A note with the photo read: "You were correct. BUT, it's not a crime to put water into an old beaver dam and it's not worth prosecuting someone for stealing water. No crime so no investigation. But we did change the ignition key for the water trucks. No harm no foul. Thanks for the help."

Noonan chuckled and turned to his wife.

"What was in the packet, dear?" she asked.

"Oh, nothing important. Just a photograph of someone putting water into a beaver pond." He showed her the photo.

"Why would anyone put water into a beaver pond? I mean, it already has water there."

"Absolutely," Noonan replied. "Do you know what the beaver said when he went into the bar?"

"A bar joke, eh? No, I don't know."

"Shut the door."

THE MATTER OF THE OOSIK ULU

Captain Heinz Noonan, the "Bearded Holmes" of the Sandersonville Police Department, was savoring the first Alaska king salmon fillet of his vacation at JENS' in Anchorage when he was tapped on the shoulder by none other than Jens himself, a Danish chief with a flair for European cuisine with an Alaskan twist.

"You aaare the eminent criminologist Captain Heinz Noonan?"

Noonan nodded that he was.

"You have no idea how I hate to break into a repast such as this but, alas, when the police call," he spread his arms in helplessness, "what can I do but comply?"

"The police called for me here? I'm on vacation."

"Perhaps. But it was the Anchorage Police and, you know, many of them stop right here and dine." He spread his arms, again, to indicate helplessness and to indicate he had no choice but to comply as the Anchorage Police were not only the representatives of law and order but some of his most sacred clients as well.

"I see. And exactly what do the Anchorage Police want?" Noonan quickly reached for his glass of wine knowing full well he had better finish it immediately because once he was lured to the phone, it could be eons before he returned to his dinner.

But Jens, the master of propriety that he was, was not to deny the Anchorage Police Department their man or a patron his dinner. With elegance and flare he quickly lifted the plate of sautéed salmon from beneath Noonan's nose and, with the other, secured the Detective's glass of wine. "The phone is in this direction," he said as he stepped toward the door leading past the wine counter. "And I will set the table for you in front of the phone so you will not miss a moment of your meal."

"But my family," sputtered Noonan as he rose, helpless but to follow.

"Not a problem," replied Jens. "I have ordered a special dessert for the family and, of course," he said looking at Lorlei Noonan who was softening as he spoke, "I have ordered a flaming plum pudding, a specialty of the house."

Otto and Fritz, the twins were busy devouring their duck *sotto nete* and clearly could have cared less what kind of a phone call dad had to receive. This was actually a victory because they usually only ate hamburgers or pizza – and often together. Lorlei nodded her assent, as if she had any power to keep her husband from answering an inquiry from the police – from any city – and went back to her *porcino con fungi*.

"This way," Jens indicated with the captain's wine glass.

Out of the main room of the restaurant and down the hall past the kitchen and the restrooms, Jens led the way to his office. A table cloth had already been spread on his desk but there were suspicious lumps which indicated the desk had not been fully cleared before the table cloth draped. Jens had thoughtfully placed a yellow dog and pencil beside the phone, just in case the captain needed to take notes. Noonan swiveled the desk chair so he could sit as Jens placed his plate on the cloth. Then, in a whirl of efficiency, the man was gone. Noonan sighed, took a swallow of Pinot Noir and picked up the receiver.

"Let me guess," he said. "You have a problem that just can't wait until morning."

"Well, actually it can," came the woman's voice. "But I was told you were planning on going salmon fishing tomorrow and wouldn't be available for a couple of days at the very least."

"That's as correct as I could have made it before I got this call."

"Yes, sir. I can understand that. Except that, well, my Commissioner . . ."

"I know. I know," replied Noonan as he rolled his eyes. "Your Commissioner called my Commissioner and in the name of inter-state law enforcement harmony, yadda, yadda, yadda."

"Yes, sir. You've said it so much better than I."

"Well, let's get to the nubbins. Whacha got?"

"Basically we've got a body of an Eskimo woman found near Barrow frozen solid with an oosik-handled ulu jammed into her ribs. She's dressed in a winter parka and traditional dress, everything except her shoes. She's wearing bunny boots. Uh, do you know what bunny boots are?" The woman's voice paused for a moment. "Or what an ulu is?"

"Hey, I'm no *cheechako*," snapped Noonan. "Bunny boots are those inflated, rubberized winter items that look like Mickey Mouse shoes and an ulu is a curved knife made to be held in one hand for lateral cutting motion as well as the more traditional cutting and hacking."

"You *do* know Alaska."

"No. I married an Alaskan."

"I see."

"Well, what's the problem?"

"The coroner says the body's at least 800 years old."

Noonan scratched his head as he looked over the body. It had been a long flight to Barrow, three hours north of Anchorage on the shore of the Arctic Ocean and then an hour helicopter ride to an ancient *barabara* where an archeological team was standing about waiting for the Coast Guard to bring in John Law. It was a pleasant day, even for a *cheechako*, a tenderfoot Alaskan, and he actually enjoyed the opportunity to be as far north on the North American continent as one could get without stepping onto shorefast ice – of which there was none this time of year.

Noonan crawled through the collapsed whale rib bone arches of the *barabara* [a sod igloo] following VPSO [Village Public Safety Officer] Geraldine Ferguson. The structure itself had collapsed centuries earlier and only through the efforts of modern day archaeologists and structural engineers was it able to be raised. The frozen sod from the room had been removed to allow access to the central chamber of the barabara. The glint of the sun's rays sparkled off the ice crystals which clung to the walls of the pit. When Noonan and Ferguson finally stood erect in the center of the pit, their feet splashed in ice-cold water, proof that the permafrost crust had been disturbed.

The body was lying on its side, face away from the two law enforcement personnel, half frozen in the bottom of the *barabara*. One arm was up over the cadaver's face as if it was shielding itself from a falling beam. The knees were drawn up until the body was in a fetal position with its feet slightly elevated. There were bunny boots on her feet, their carefully laced knots frozen solid with ice.

"There's the ulu," Ferguson said as she pointed to the embedded object in the fold of the woman's parka. "It has an oosik handle and you can see the rivets holding the steel plate in place."

"There wasn't a lot of steel around here 800 years ago – if your coroner is accurate in his estimate of eon of death."

"The earliest there could have been steel around here was the mid-1700s, two and a half centuries ago." Ferguson splashed to another angle and pulled out a camera with a flash attachment. "I've got to take photographs for the crime lab," she smiled. "You know, crime scene stuff."

Noonan nodded and moved sideways as she snapped the photograph. Being careful to stay out of her photographs, he looked down at the face of the corpse. It had a desiccated look, the skin pulled back tight against the cheek and chin bones. The neck was short and disappeared into the fur seal collar of the parka. The body was wrapped in the parka almost as if it were a blanket which covered the entire body except for the short expanse of legs to which the bunny boots were attached.

He splashed over to the body and snapped on a flash light. In its halo he examined the ulu carefully, from its handle to the blade which had been driven deep into the woman's ribs.

If there was any blood, it had either been washed away as the ice crystals had melted or it had long ago soaked into the fine black fur of the parka.

"Yes, this certainly is an interesting find," Noonan commented as he stood up and stepped back from the corpse.

"Well, what do you think?" Ferguson rolled her film forward as she joined Noonan beside the corpse.

"Well, I'll say it's an interesting case. Where's the nearest modern day village from here?"

"Kaktovik? Oh, I'd say about six miles away. To the west. It's a small village of about 200."

"How do they make their living?"

"Subsistence mostly, why?"

"Anything unusual been happening there lately?"

"Well, the oil industry used to hire quite a few of the Natives but since the downturn of the oil business there hasn't been any real work. It's typical of a lot of Native communities. They do some trapping, some fishing, some hunting."

"Tourism?"

"Every once in a while someone stops by, yeah, but other than that, no."

Noonan began working his way back toward the front of the *barabara*. "I imagine that will change when news of this gets out."

"Maybe. This is a long way from any place."

"You don't know the American press."

Clearly Ferguson didn't. By the time they crawled out of the *barabara*, there were two film crews getting off a helicopter, CNN and NBC. One of the crews had zeroed in on the coroner, clearly visible in his white uniform with the words CORONER,

CITY OF KAKTOVIK on his back. The other crew was getting establishing shots of the crumbling *barabara*.

Noonan didn't give the camera crews more than a glance as he walked directly toward the Coast Guard helicopter. When one of the newswomen from NBC tried to catch his attention, Noonan just waved politely. Then he and the VPSO boarded the helicopter. "OK!" Noonan shouted above the roar of the blades. "Let's rock and roll." Five seconds later they were aloft.

"Well look who returns from the frozen north," Jens said gleefully as Captain Noonan wandered into JENS'. "I see you are back from the shore of the Arctic Ocean. But I didn't see you on the evening news. Did the camera crews miss you?"

"Ah, Jens. It's so nice to be back. I did enjoy the trip, by the way, and I certainly appreciate your thoughtfulness."

"Eh?" said Jens in surprise.

"The corpse. An elegant touch, I might add. Quite elegant indeed. A classic case of Alaskan absurding."

"So you saw through our little charade did you? My, but you are a clever man, you are, Captain Heinz Noonan."

"You Alaskans think you're so clever. Really. An oosik-handled ulu. That was so poor, Jens. Really, from a man with as fine-tuned a mind as you have."

"It was the thought that counted," replied Jens as he smiled.

"But I must admit that it would probably have fooled a *cheechako*," replied Noonan. "Someone who didn't know there are no seal and walrus in the Arctic Ocean. I knew from the start that it was a fake. But I was intrigued. Bunny boots? Really?"

"I guess that might have been a bit much."

"A bit much? Jens, everything was a bit much. Unless you're not an Alaskan. I've been married to an Alaskan for a decade, remember? And that was a very dry corpse. You probably picked it out of some pawn shop or some sort of curio establishment – if it's real at all. And the fur seal parka? Really! No Eskimo would be wearing a parka inside a *barabara*. More important, fur seal is from the Bering Sea, what, a thousand miles away!"

Jens smiled mischievously and bowed.

"But what I liked best, of course, was the Kaktovik Coroner. Give me a break, Jens. That's a village of 200. I know towns of 250,000 that don't have a coroner. The white lab coat was a piece of work, however, a true work of genius."

Jens smiled. "So you liked that?" Jens smiled as Noonan smiled. "Good! Then the press corps will love it too."

"Indeed I did. I imagine it was all to generate some tourism into Kaktovik. Perhaps a little bit of excitement for an otherwise dull summer?"

"Ah, you see through me like glass, Captain. The summer has been a bit dull and some of the executives from one of the Native corporations wanted to liven things up with some good old Alaskan absurding. You know, pass off something absolutely absurd as the truth and see how long it takes Outsiders to catch on."

"I'm not your typical Outsider. I may live in the Lower 48 but I'm not *cheechako*."

"That you're not. I actually expected you to be on the evening news. What tipped you?"

"Jens!" Noonan stepped back and spread his arms as he turned in a tight circle in the center of the restaurant. "Just how did VPSO Ferguson know to call me here?"

[*Author's note*: If you knew the body was a hoax when the oosik was first mentioned, you are a sourdough. If you didn't catch the hoax until the fur seal parka was mentioned, you're a *cheechako* but there's hope for you. If you were convinced the coroner for Kaktovik was real, the author has some beach front property in Talkeetna for sale at a very modest price. But if it took you until the end of the story, you should contact the Alaska Division of Tourism.]

THE MATTER OF THE
VEGETARIAN ANACONDA

Captain Noonan, the "Bearded Holmes" of the Sandersonville Police Department, was well into his second cup of coffee of the morning, vicious though it was without his usually generous helpings of cream and sugar. It was not that the weight monster was ruthless attacking him, rather the Christmas season was upon him and he anticipated numerous gatherings at which he would be expected to consume fattening substances. This he considered was not only a God-given right but a political necessity. The former he relished while the latter he detested. Overall, he didn't object to the ingesting, just the aftermath in January when he would have to increase his visits to the gym and reduce his carbo-rich diet at his favorite Italian restaurant, Lorenzo's.

Coffee without the usually rich helpings of cream and sugar was not the pleasure he anticipated so he ceased imbibing at the second sip. Actually, before the second sip. Then he set the cup down which, in this instance, was fortunate as the phone rang as his cup made contact with the table.

"Noonan," he said as he picked up the receiver.

"Captain Noonan?"

"Better be," replied the detective. "Or I'm paying someone else's bills."

There was a chuckle on the other end of the line. "I'm paying enough bills for both of us so maybe this is your lucky day."

"The last time I had a lucky day my wife came home from shopping empty-handed because she had lost her wallet."

"Did she ever find it?"

"You mean where I hid it under the sofa cushion to discourage her from going shopping at all? Yeah, about five minutes after she got home."

"Then she went back to the mall?"

"Broke a nail trying to get the key into the ignition too fast. I had to pay for that too."

The male voice chuckled again. "Well, I'm glad you've got a sense of humor because I've got a doozy of a case here. I'm Detective David Solomon in Riverside, California . . ."

"Home of the Mission Inn, right?"

"You got it. Orange capital of the world. Except for Florida and Hawaii and a whole bunch of other places."

"Yeah. I've been there. I was at a conference there last year."

"That's right. That's why I'm calling. My Chief met you . . ."

"That's the way these things always start. I hope it's a bizarre case because, frankly, I haven't had a good whodunit in a while."

"I heard you specialized in strange cases and this one, I've got to say, is very different."

"How different?"

"Let's see. We've got a vegetarian anaconda, two clowns, three *bichon frise* and . . ."

". . . a partridge in a pear tree?"

"Close enough for this season. We've got five antique rings and a *faux* Fabergé egg."

"Quite a collection. Am I supposed to believe it?"

"Unfortunately, I hope so. If I hadn't been a party to the events, I wouldn't have believed it either."

"There is a crime involved in this, right? I'd hate to work my brain for a practical joke."

"Oh, there's a crime here. At least we think there is. We're talking about five antique, one-of-a-kind rings that are collectively worth about $20,000.

"I've worked on stranger cases. Let's hear what you've got."

"The story is a bit strange."

"What a surprise!"

"Putting the pieces together slowly, it appears there were two robberies at the same time in two different parts of Riverside. We know both are related because both robbers hit the stores dressed as clowns. They were a real Mutt-and-Jeff outfit, if you can use that term to describe two people not together. One was well over six foot six and the other might have been five feet tall."

"You sure they were on the same team, so to speak?"

"Absolutely. They were both dressed as clowns, stayed in the stores less than 90 seconds, came on foot, escaped on foot, both used pistols, both had heavy face make-up."

"Were the costumes similar?"

"Other than they were in clown outfits, no."

"Then this could be one heck of a coincidence."

"We don't think so. Both clowns left a rubber chicken with the same note. The notes read, 'I'll be back.'" Detective Solomon read the word "back" as if Arnold Schwarzenegger would have said it "bahhhk."

"Sound conclusive to me."

"That's the way we looked at it too. But the taking of the rings was strange. They were antiques and had all been insured. That means all of the rings had been fingerprinted, if that's the correct term for rings."

"Close enough. You mean that all of the diamonds in the rings had been spectrographed so if they turn up again, you'd know it."

"Right. So the jewelry is easily traceable. The thief knew what he were doing. He actually took the traceable rings and left the real valuable stuff alone."

"Whoa! You said 'he.' Do you know it was a he? And you used the term in the singular."

"Actually no one knows the sex of either clown. They didn't speak. They just arrived with guns, took what they wanted and left. There were two robberies. One was the jewelry store and the other was an antique store. At the antique store, all that was taken was the *faux* Faberge' egg."

"A fake one, humm. What's the worth?"

"Maybe $500."

"Is there any connection between the antique rings and this *faux*" – Noonan accented the term as if it were a gourmet French *pate'* – "Faberge' egg?"

"Other than the clown robbers, not that we can see."

"I'm waiting for the vegetarian anaconda. I know this is a crazy question but was there a circus in town at the moment?"

"Yes, there was, and is, as a matter of fact. That's the reason the robbery went so smoothly. We've had clowns and ballerinas all over town hyping the circus so a clown on the street was no big deal. But neither of the clowns were from the circus. We checked. From the midgets to the thin man. We also checked with the last three cities where the circus performed. No robberies remotely similar to these."

"I'm dying to hear about the vegetarian anaconda."

"That's where the story gets more bizarre."

"Oh, do tell."

"The two robberies were held at the same time. And I mean the same time, the same 90 seconds. The perps grabbed two cabs for the circus. It's down town so the cabbies didn't know they were carrying thieves. We found out about 30 minutes later. Both cabs went to the same location, the kennels for the *bichon frise*. Those are . . ."

"Yeah. I know. Those are the little white dogs that do all the circus tricks."

"You are amazing well-educated in circus lore."

"No. My brother-in-law has two of them."

"Oh. OK. At the *Frise* kennels the pair dumped their disguises. They clearly knew what they were doing because the *Frise* kennels are the only ones in the circus that have an open flame for heating."

"Sorry?"

"Heating. The circus is in a huge tent that's heated. All of the crew and the animals are housed in vans and tents behind the main circus tent. When it gets cold this time of year the animals are kept in their heated vans until they are ready to perform. But there are a number of 55-gallon drums around the compound that have open fires in them. That's to keep the crew warm when they're working outside. One of those drums is near the *Frise* kennels. Apparently, the dogs don't care one way or the other about an open flame."

"So the perps dropped their disguises into the fire in the drum?"

"Yup. By the time we found them, there wasn't much left. Not enough for a DNA match anyway and the fiber evidence, pfffffft! A clown in a circus is invisible, so to speak. Once they pulled off their costumes they could blend in with the crowd and be invisible in another sense."

"Any other evidence at the *Frise* kennels?"

"Lots and lots of footprints."

"I would have suspected that."

"Then we got the call about the vegetarian anaconda."

"This I have been waiting to hear."

"Whether by accident or circumstance, our perps made it into the serpentine through an unlocked door. It's really warm in there, you know, with all those reptiles."

"Just snakes?"

"The circus isn't that large so there aren't that many. The big one, of course, is the anaconda. It's about 15 feet long and about as active as a dead tree in a swamp."

"Unless it's feeding time."

"That's right. Speaking of feeding, this particular anaconda has a metabolic difficulty. It can't digest raw meat with any efficiency so the zookeepers have been feeding it a mixture of things of vegetarian foodstuffs all gooed together to be made to look like a small animal. Then they wrap the goo in rat skin . . . ."

"Rat skin?"

"Yeah. They skin a bunch of house rats and use the skin to surround the vegetarian goo. It fools the snake into thinking it's eating a rat. At least it must because it's working. The snake eats what it thinks is a rat. Apparently, it doesn't have taste buds to clue it otherwise. Whatever. The anaconda has been eating the vegetarian gunk and gaining weight."

"Is there a reason you're telling me about the vegetarian anaconda?"

"There is. We suspected that the perps put the *faux* Faberge' egg into the vegetarian goo and the anaconda swallowed it. We're not sure if the perps hid the loot in the goo and were planning on coming back or expected the anaconda to swallow the haul so they could, er, retrieve it at a later date."

"I see. How did you know that the anaconda swallowed the loot?"

"The snake was having digestive problems the day after the robbery so the vet took an X-ray and, poof, there was a metal obstruction. So the vet operated."

"He found the stolen egg?"

"Nope. He found the gold rings. The egg is still missing."

"Let me get this straight. You were following the Mutt-and-Jeff act after the theft of the *faux* Faberge' egg worth all of, what $500, and found $20,000 worth of rings?"

"That's the size of it. The reason I'm calling you is to ask, 'What's going on here?'"

"Now *that* is a good question." Noonan thought for a moment and then said. "I've got some preliminary questions."

"Shoot."

"How much press coverage has the vegetarian anaconda received? Were both the robberies caught on security cameras?

How far apart were the two robberies? Who was actually in the stores when the robberies occurred? Which robbery did the tall perp pull off? Are you sure the Faberge' egg is *faux*? Were the egg and/or the rings insured? Did you do a background check on the owners of the rings? Is there any connection between the antique store owner and the jewelry store owner? How long has the circus been in town? Where did you look for the egg at the circus? Does anyone at either store have a criminal record?"

"Some of that information I have. The two robberies were exactly a mile apart. I know that because the jewelry store was on the corner of Main and First and the other was at Main and Fourteenth. At 14 city blocks to a mile, that makes them exactly a mile apart. Both stores were hit early in the day. There were no customers in the jewelry store at the time and that robbery was caught on video. I've seen it. The tall perp comes in and waves the clerks – two of them – onto the floor. The perp walks behind the counter and pops open a drawer, the whole time holding the clerks down on the ground with a pistol. Then he's gone. Under 90 seconds. The instant the perp is out the door, the clerks are up and calling the police."

"No alarm?"

"No. That alarm is activated by the clerks. Since the robbery was over they just called 911."

"The perp went right for the rings? He didn't look around and then decide to go for the antique rings."

"He went right for the rings. Straight for them. As soon as we got there we got the names of the owners and ran them through NCIC. Got some solid hits, interesting but nothing punishing. One is owned by an old lady in Victorville, a town in the desert, who wants to give the ring to her granddaughter.

The second ring is owned by a retired underworld character who's been clean for 40 years. He lives in Las Vegas. The other two rings come from a large jewelry operation in San Diego. The rings were in Riverside on consignment. The rings were actually owned by two people and here's where it gets interesting. One is part of Al Capone's jewelry collection that has just been liquidated. It was a pinky ring and was purchased by an organized crime figure on parole. He swears he had nothing to do with the robbery but we're not sure. He lives in Arizona and the Tucson Police are keeping an eye on him. The other ring is owned by a small antique jewelry cooperative run by a couple that has, collectively, records that include money laundering, receiving stolen property, extortion, obstruction of justice and retail fraud running back to three decades."

"Where does that couple live?"

"Right now. Phoenix. But they lived in San Francisco recently and were briefly considered suspects in a major diamond robbery in Denver. But they were eliminated, reluctantly I was told, because they were not in Denver at the time."

"Do you have any detail about that robbery?"

"Not that the Denver Police would release. Just what was in the newspaper. A diamond merchant was robbed of about a million in gems. No one was hurt and the insurance company paid off. The diamonds were probably cut up because none have surfaced."

"Why was the couple suspected?"

"Jewelry is an incestuous business. It takes a chunk of change to get started, particularly if it's a small operation. So everyone knows everyone else and there is trading of jewelry on consignments, mixing and matching of antiques. That kind of thing. Their name came up on paperwork which, surprisingly, turned out to be legitimate."

"How about the underworld figure in Las Vegas?"

"In his 90s. Used to be, or, rather, alleged to have been, a torpedo for Al Capone, interestingly. He's still ambulatory so the Las Vegas police are watching him."

"How about the egg?"

"Just a *faux* Faberge' egg. It pops open to show a carriage. It looks good from far away. It wasn't insured, by the way."

"What's a *faux* Faberge' egg doing in an antique store?"

"Part of an estate sale. 'Antique' is a nice way of referring to that store, by the way. I'd call it more of a high-class oddity shop. It's got some good stuff but the owner doesn't have a lot of money so he's moving anything he can get. He's got some high-priced painting from local legends, 20s furniture, lots of heirloom jewelry but nothing into the $10,000 and above range. He's been in business in Riverside for a decade. No record. There's no business connection between the antique store and the jewelry store that got robbed. But it's hard to believe the owners don't know each other. Both are active in the Downtown Business Association and other nonprofits."

"Does the antique store have a security camera?"

"No. It's a small operation. The perp, the short one, came in with a gun just as the store opened. The perp duct taped the owner, took the egg and vanished. His wife found him half an hour later. That was when we knew we had two robberies."

"How long has the circus been in town?"

"Two weeks. It has another week to run. I don't know anything about the vegetarian anaconda so that information I'll have to research. I can't remember if there was another question."

"Where did you look for the egg at the circus?"

"We did a search but I wouldn't call it thorough. There have been crowds there 15 hours a day."

"Does the outside crew at the circus feed the animals?"

"I presume so."

"Do any animals there eat an oat or barley mix? Something that would have to be fed with a shovel."

"I don't know. I'll find out."

"Don't bother. Look for that *faux* Faberge' egg in the animal feed mix. Make sure it's not a real Faberge's egg and then hold onto it for the moment. Were the rings returned?"

"Not yet."

"Hang onto them too."

"OK. Any other questions?"

"A couple of more. See if you can get any more information on the heist in Denver. Was it ever solved? If not, exactly what was stolen? Also see what else was in the Capone liquidation."

"You mean, like a *faux* Faberge' egg?"

"It crossed my mind. And don't forget the press coverage for the vegetarian anaconda."

"You really like that, don't you?"

"I've never heard of a vegetarian snake."

"I'll see what I can do."

Three hours later and yet another attempt at black coffee, Noonan got another call from Riverside.

"I have some good news and bad news."

"Let me guess. The good news is that you found the egg; it's the faux egg as identified by the antique store owner. The bad news is that everything else is a dead end."

"You've been here before."

"Sort of. Where did you find the egg?"

"In an oat mix for the elephant. It wasn't that hard to find once we started digging into the feed mix."

"I kind of thought that would be the case. About the anaconda?"

"There has been quite a bit of press coverage. This is the only vegetarian anaconda on earth and the local papers went into quite a bit of detail on the snake. I've got all kinds of information on the vegetarian goo. Do you want that?"

"No. What did it say about how the snake is handled?"

"Just that it is carefully watched because it is so valuable as the world's only vegetarian anaconda. It is X-rayed frequently to make certain nothing is going wrong inside and it consumes lots of rat skins. It also gave a feeding schedule for local vets."

"How about that Denver robbery?"

"Nothing has turned up. I asked what was stolen and I was told it was about a handful of gems if the certificate of authenticities and individual envelopes were eliminated. Quite a haul though."

"I'll bet."

"Don't keep me in suspense! If you knew where the egg was to be found, you know what happened."

"Maybe. I'm a long way from where you are but I think the reason you're having a hard time making sense of what is going on is because there are two different robbery scenarios at the same time, one of which never happened."

"Huh?"

"First of all, your clown robberies were probably staged. Here's what I think happened. The owner of the antique store disguised himself as a clown and put on some kind short stilts. He didn't have to be too good on the stilts because he was only acting for the security camera. By being seen on the security camera as about six foot six that would put him in the clear and lead the police to look for a tall man who never existed."

"But the short thief?"

"Never existed. The only person who saw the short thief was the antique store owner. I'll bet his wife dressed up as the short clown and took a cab to the *bichon frise* kennels at a specific moment, just in time to meet her husband. She could not have been caught because she had not reported the robbery of the antique store yet. She might have even had some business cards in her pocket just in case she was stopped so she could say she was advertising the shop. Since she owned the *faux* Faberge' egg, it wasn't stolen."

"If that's the case, why did she report the egg stolen?"

"I'll get to that in a moment. When she got to the *bichon frise* kennels, she stripped off her disguise and dropped it in the open fire. Thus she accounted for the second clown. She took the egg and deposited it somewhere it would remain safe and still be found intact. The most logical place was a feed box or pile where it would be discovered when the animals were fed sometime during the week. The egg you found, by the way, is not the egg that was allegedly stolen. I'll get into that in a minute."

"But, but . . ."

"Let me finish. While she was hiding the egg, her husband dressed as a clown took a cab to the *bichon frise* kennel. I'll bet when you check the 911 call you'll see there is a gap between the time the robbery occurred and the call was made. That was to give the perp time to get to the kennels and burn the costume. Once the second costume was being burned, there went the proof of both robberies. The perp may have even used a cell phone to call the jewelry store to say he was in the clear."

"Why did they need two robberies?"

"Because there were, in fact, three crimes and the two robberies were meant to cover up the third."

"I'm lost."

"OK. Let's take this backwards. Think of the two clown robberies. We'll call them the clown robberies. Everything that was stolen was recovered. There was no insurance loss. Those robberies were simply designed to create a distraction. They did their job well. You investigated all kinds of people who had nothing to do with the clown robberies. You found the rings in the vegetarian anaconda. You were meant to find the rings. The perps knew the anaconda was going to be X-rayed so they knew the rings would be found. They knew the egg would be found as well. When the rings and egg were found, the police would think the robberies were a prank. No loss, no crime. Even if you caught the clowns the antique store couple and the jewelry store owner would have called it a publicity stunt. There wouldn't be much you could do because if nothing was stolen, no insurance collected."

"Rrrr-ight. But why did they do it?"

"Because there was a second robbery in progress at the same time. Remember that heist in Denver?"

"For a million in loose gems, yeah."

"Well, I'm betting the rings were a distraction from the *faux* Faberge' egg. The egg had no value so the police wouldn't care about it. But someone else would. It wasn't the egg that was valuable. It was what was inside. I'll bet there were a million dollars' worth of diamonds in that egg, the million from the Denver heist. Here's what I think happened. Your fine couple in Phoenix is the fence for those Denver diamonds. But they can't take them directly. They need a paper trail. So they contacted the jeweler there in Riverside. I'll bet he's small. He may be crooked but he's still small. He could leak the stones out slowly enough to allay any suspicion but he couldn't put them in his inventory. That many stones was too risky. So he subcontracted, so to speak, to the antiques dealer. There isn't a record problem with antiques dealers. It's a cash and carry kind of business. That was how the diamond deal was supposed to work. The gems from the heist would slowly go through the antiques dealer books to the Riverside jeweler to the Phoenix couple with the Riversiders taking an administrative fee. Everyone would have paper on the gems just in case the police got nosey."

"That still doesn't tell me how the egg is involved."

"The diamonds came to the antique dealer in the *faux* egg. But not the egg you have in your hand. The diamonds went into a *faux* egg and that egg went to the antiques dealer to start the process."

"How do you know that?"

"Because there is no other reason for the egg to have been stolen. It was stolen to make the Phoenix couple believe that the diamonds had been stolen in an elaborate robbery. That way the diamonds disappear. Someone stole them from the antiques dealer. As long as the antiques dealer doesn't get suddenly wealthy, the Phoenix couple is out $1 million in diamonds and can't find them. The stealing of the egg was to convince the Phoenix couple the egg had been stolen and therefore, by extension, the diamonds had been stolen as well."

"If that was true, why was the egg recovered?"

"The real perps, the antiques dealer couple and the jeweler need to show the Phoenix couple they don't have the diamonds. If the egg just disappears, there will always be the suspicion that the Phoenix couple was double-crossed. If the egg turns up and is empty, that suspicion goes away. I'll bet that the antiques dealer will figure out some way to pop the figurine in the egg out to show you the egg is empty. He might even give it to the local museum as a donation. Anything to get a line in the newspaper that the egg is empty. Ergo the diamonds have been stolen."

"Then the antiques dealer and the jeweler can sell the stones slowly and keep the profits for themselves."

"Yup. The rings were stolen to draw attention to the egg. The egg was stolen to double-cross the Phoenix couple. The vegetarian anaconda was used because it was X-rayed frequently which meant the rings would be found quickly. Once the rings and the egg were found, the case would go cold. It was a very clever scheme because if either of the clowns had been caught at any point during the alleged robbery, there was a logical explanation. Thus there would have been no crime."

"Well, where are the diamonds?"

"I'd say the antiques dealer still has them. I'm betting that they are still in a *faux* Faberge' egg, possibly even out in the open in a display case. He probably has a collection of them. The jeweler can't keep the diamonds because he's subject to audits. I'll bet if you searched the antique dealers store you'd find the diamonds."

"We can't do that without a warrant."

"True. But you can make everyone's life miserable by returning the egg to the dealer without letting him pop it open. Have him identify it and just give it back. Tell the press it was returned unopened and make sure they write it up that way. Then keep a very sharp eye on the antiques dealer because things will start popping right away. That Phoenix couple is going to figure out they are being double-crossed. If they get really mad, you could get all the fish in one net."

"Everything makes sense but I'll have to think about it. But I like the way you think. By the way, what tipped you? Was there any one thing?"

"Well, a couple of things. First, why should the clowns bother to leave notes? And particularly ones that said they would be bahhhhk." Noonan said "back" like Arnold Schwarzenegger. "There was no reason. Ergo, the notes were to definitively link the two robberies – as if the clown outfits were not enough. Then there was the description of the second clown, the alleged one. The dealer described the perp as five feet tall. There are not that many people that small and that raised my suspicion. You can make someone appear taller but not shorter. Since the taller perp was caught on the security camera and the short one wasn't, that solidified my suspicions that the short one never existed. If one perp didn't exist, then why invent him? To give the second perp credibility. My conclusion was the clown robberies were for not for profit – and there is no such a thing as a robbery that does not involve profit for someone. So, there must have been a second robbery for profit somewhere in the background."

"So you found the money and followed it."

"Right. When you don't know what to do, follow the money. I did. Now I want to make sure the perps end up with egg on their face, so to speak."

"That was a cruel pun."

"Not as cruel as what will likely happen when the Phoenix couple comes to Riverside. They do not sound like pleasant people. You might have antiques couple and the jeweler knocking on your door with a confession."

"Now that's my kind of a happy ending."

"Snakes alive!" Noonan said. "It's time for me to slither out of here!"

"Well," came the reply, "thanks for the help and I'll snake on down to a press conference. Who knows? If I can speak enough truth with a forked tongue I might be able to draw someone out of their snake's den."

"Don't take any tofu rats, though. I hear they are hell on the digestive system. A lot like black coffee." And with that, the Chief of Detectives of the Sandersonville Police Department hung up.

THE MATTER OF THE
NONEXISTENT ADDRESS

Captain Heinz Noonan, the "Bearded Holmes" of the Sandersonville Police Department, was sitting in the Alaska Airlines courtesy lounge in the Seattle -Tacoma Airport when he got the call. Calls always seemed to come at the most inappropriate instant, usually just when he had other things to do. In this case, he was waiting to catch the 9:45 a.m. shuttle to San Francisco -- and Alaska Airlines had an annoying habit of being on time.

"Captain Noonan," a smooth, generic female voice flowed mellifluously over the loudspeaker. "Will you please take Line 5? Captain Noonan, will you please take Line 5. Thank you very much."

"I didn't lose it," Noonan mumbled angrily as he lunged toward the phone. Looking at the office memo in his hand he re-read that his wife had called at 9:00 a.m. asking about the invitation to the luncheon that afternoon. "I *distinctly* remember telling her it was in the bin on top of the computer hard drive, where we put all our invitations. If she hadn't been on the line 20 minutes ago this would have all be cleared up."

"I didn't lose it," he snapped when he picked up Line 5.

There was a split-second of silence on the line and then a middle-aged female voice responded, "Maybe not but we lost $150,000 in gems."

"Excuse me," Noonan said at the unexpected voice, "I thought it was my wife calling. How did you know I was at the airport?"

"Your wife told me. How else? This is Lt. Carey with the Boston Police Department. We've got a bit of a problem that is time critical, as they say."

"When it comes to crime, everything is time critical."

"Uh, yes, Sir. You are quite right. Your name was given to me by Captain O'Reilly who attended a talk you gave last year at the DSO Academy."

"I remember the talk but not your Captain."

"He didn't come forward with his congratulations. But he did think highly enough of you to suggest I call the Sandersonville Police Department and talk with you. They were kind enough to give me your home phone and your wife told me where you could be reached."

"I'll bet she did," mumbled Noonan to himself.

"Sorry?"

"Nothing, Lt. What can I do for the Boston Police Department?" He paused for a second. "And please be brief because I'm about to catch a flight to San Francisco."

"Yes, sir. Well, we have a case involving $150,000 in lost gems and we have every reason to believe that if we move fast we'll catch the perps before they flee the city."

"The Boston Police is the one of the best in the country. Why do you need me?"

"First, because I'm the highest ranking officer on duty today. It's my watch and I'm responsible for the city today. Second, we've got exits to the city covered but, frankly, we need an edge. You, quite frankly sir, would be quite an edge to have."

"I see. I don't know that I can do that much but give me what you have."

"Yes, sir. The Burlington Gem and Diamond Exchange made a delivery in Cambridge late last night. The delivery man made the delivery on time at 325 Third Street. He went to the third floor, knocked on the door to Room 307, got the password and was shown the proper credentials. He got a signature and left."

"Ah," said Noonan knowingly. "Now, let me guess. The next morning you got a call from the Burlington Gem and Diamond Exchange. The delivery order was a phony."

"That's right, Captain Noonan. We immediately went with the delivery man to 325 Third Street and . . ."

". . . and there was a vacant lot at 325 Third, or the building didn't have a third floor, or it was an aquarium."

"You got it right on the first guess. It was a vacant lot."

Before Noonan had a chance to reply the boarding call for the 9:45 flight blared overhead.

"I just got the call for my flight," Noonan said hurriedly. "Let me just ask you a couple of more questions. First, was the delivery man new to the Boston area?"

"He'd been in the area for about three years. Came here from California. We checked him out with the company and former employers if that's what you're getting at. His record is clean. Eagle Scout and Congressional Medal of Honor Winner. No dirt there."

"The Burlington end is legit?"

"As far as we know. Old, established company. Been around the Boston area for over 60 years. No robberies. No losses. Family-owned. No financial problems we can find. In fact, the robbery is going to hurt them more than $150,000 worth."

"OK. Tell me about Cambridge. I've only been there once."

"Old town. Home of Harvard University. Founded by John Harvard and local farmers in the 1760s and grew up around the local farms. Main street into town is MassAve – and that's pronounced like it's one word, by the way. Streets wander all over the place along both sides of MassAve. Third Street is broken into all kinds of little pieces across Cambridge, sometimes changing names but it's still the same street. But before you leap to any conclusions, 325 Third is in the third block back from MassAve. He couldn't, and swears he didn't, have made that mistake. He swears he could even see MassAve from the address."

"Do you believe him?"

"No sign of drugs in his bloodstream. Yeah, I believe him."

"Who do you think's got the diamonds?"

"Hard to say. We've got a couple of locals we're watching but the Number One suspect is holed up somewhere."

The last boarding call sounded and Noonan rose suddenly. "I can't talk any more, Lt. I've got to catch that plane. Look, call me at the San Francisco airport and . . ."

"Do you want me to call you on the plane?"

"No. I need time to think."

"OK. I'll call you at San Francisco International, in the Alaska Airlines courtesy lounge."

"Fine. I'll expect your call there."

Three hours later Captain Noonan was seated in the Alaska Airlines courtesy lounge in San Francisco. Noonan picked up the courtesy phone and placed a call to Boston. "Now, Lt. Carey. Let me ask a few more questions. How did your delivery man get to Cambridge?"

"He took the subway to Harvard Square and then walked to Third Avenue."

"About how far is that?"

"Half mile, maybe less. The street doesn't make it a straight shot."

"Did he have a map?"

"Not a taxi cab map, if that's what you mean. But he did have a city map of Boston."

"Was it one of those maps where Cambridge was a little square on the back of the map while Boston covered the whole other side?"

"That would be my guess. Do you want me to ask?"

"No. I think I've got it figured out. Is your lab team ready? If you're going to catch these perps you're going to have to go over Room 307 with a fine tooth comb."

"When we find the room."

"Don't worry. You will. Get your lab team to Harvard Square, where the delivery man came out of the subway, the MTA. Have them go up MassAve and carefully look at every street sign all the way to Third Avenue. I'll bet they'll find that every one of them has been tampered with. If Cambridge streets are like those in Boston there's a South First Street followed a block later by North First Street which, in turn is followed by South Second Street which is followed by North Third Street."

"I don't know. I live in Plymouth."

"The delivery man probably didn't know either. He probably lived in Boston and didn't get out to Cambridge very much. That's a college town, a strange place to take a diamond delivery. I'll bet that someone changed the street signs on North and South, First, Second, and Third streets. Then, when the delivery man walked up MassAve he passed a new sign for First Street and then, maybe, a Harvard Street. The next block would have been Second Street and the following block, perhaps, Kennedy Street. Then the next block would have been labeled, oh, Peabody Street. He would have gone another block and there was Third Street which, in reality, was actually South Third Street. That's the street where he made his delivery. If you go to 325 on that street, you'll find a building with at least three stories and a room 307. That's where you want to send you lab team."

"Well, why didn't we spot this earlier?"

"You said that the delivery man was using a small map of Cambridge. It probably didn't have the north and south firsts, seconds and thirds listed. He found Third Street where he expected it and made the delivery."

"But why didn't we find it when we went back and looked this morning?"

"You said you were in charge and you lived in Plymouth. If you've never been to Cambridge you wouldn't have known the streets are numbered that way. And some of the signs were changed. Right after the delivery, the signs reading Harvard, Kennedy and Peabody came down and the Third Street sign was moved to North Third. When you went to find the building, you thought you were on Third Street. In actually you were on North Third Street. You were just one block off."

"It sounds so simple when you explain it."

"One more thing. Have you lab team pay special attention to the toilet seat lid when they dust for fingerprints."

"Really? Why?"

"Because I'm betting that this is an inside job. The man who took the delivery had to have the proper documentation. For a precious gem company, that probably means the security paperwork changes frequently. If the delivery man is straight, than there is someone at Burlington who is bent. If Burlington is an old, established firm, whoever pulled this job off was an amateur. They do things like wipe the silverware and door handles clean but often forget things like toilet seats which they raise and lower as conditions warrant."

"Good thought."

"Good hunting."

"Oh, Captain Noonan,"

"Yes."

"You were in such a hurry in Sandersonville I didn't get a chance to tell you your wife asked me to tell you she found the invitation that you lost."

"I didn't lose it!" Noonan snapped but he was speaking to a dead line.